SHADOW STATE

{Imprint} MAKE YOUR MARK

NEW YORK

ELYSE BRAYDEN

SHADOW
STATE

[Imprint]
MAKE YOUR MARK

A part of Macmillan Publishing Group, LLC
175 Fifth Avenue, New York, NY 10010

Library of Congress Control Number: 2017957969.

ISBN 978-1-250-12423-4 (hardcover) / ISBN 978-1-250-12424-1 (ebook)

Our books may be purchased in bulk for promotional, educational, or business
use. Please contact your local bookseller or the Macmillan Corporate and
Premium Sales Department at (800) 221-7945 ext. 5442 or by e-mail
at MacmillanSpecialMarkets@macmillan.com.

Book design by Liz Dresner

Imprint logo designed by Amanda Spielman

First edition, 2018

10 9 8 7 6 5 4 3 2 1

fiercereads.com

This book contains thievery and stealth—but for the greater good. If you're
thinking about stealing it, however, think again. Because eyes are on you.
What you think is real might not be. Watch your back.

TO ALL THE BRYNNS
OF THE WORLD—DON'T LET
ANYTHING OR ANYONE
BRING YOU DOWN.

AUTHOR'S NOTE

THIS NOVEL FEATURES characters dealing with depression and suicide. If you've ever felt very depressed or thought about suicide yourself, there are a lot of other people like you. But it's important that you tell someone else how you're feeling. A friend, a parent, someone at school—any of these people can help you find support.

If you don't want to talk to someone you know, there are many services that provide free, confidential help to anyone struggling with depression and suicidal thoughts.

Here's one well-known provider:

THE NATIONAL SUICIDE PREVENTION LIFELINE

The Lifeline provides free and confidential support for

people in distress, twenty-four hours a day, seven days a week. Its toll-free number is 1-800-273-8255.

Its website is suicidepreventionlifeline.org.

This book also describes a fictional drug that bears no resemblance to the actual medications used to treat psychiatric disorders. If you have any questions about the treatment of common mental health issues such as depression, anxiety, or the after-effects of trauma, including the use of medication, the best person to consult is a doctor or other health-care professional.

PROLOGUE

Brynn Caldwell sprinted as fast as she could across the walkway, the sound of her shoes ringing sharply off the hard walls and ceiling. She feared every step would be her last. She looked down at the heavy object she was struggling to hold in her arms. *Keep it together*, she willed herself. *You can do this. You have to do this.*

She continued on, sweating under a blast of hot air from a heating vent. The other side of the walkway would get her to safety. She paused, listening to the din below. The sounds were so happy—everyone drinking, eating, talking, smiling, laughing, *celebrating*. There were people she knew down there—people she loved. They had no idea she was up here. They had no idea about *anything*. Only Brynn knew what was to come—and how devastating it was going to be.

She took a deep breath and kept going. *You might not have gotten everyone into this mess,* she thought, *but it's up to you to get everyone out.*

It was all up to her now. If she didn't do something immediately, everyone down there, every last person in the crowd, would be dead within minutes.

TWELVE DAYS EARLIER

ONE

TWELVE DAYS TO LAUNCH

The large round table at the Annapolis Yacht Club was festooned with elegant china dishes, shining crystal glasses, polished silver forks and spoons, and a stunning arrangement of hydrangeas and roses. A string quartet played something baroque and soothing, and a large silver banner bearing the words THE NATIONAL DOVE CHEMICAL ENGINEER-ING AWARD hung over a tall podium. Brynn Caldwell, Dove Award nominee, sat in front of an untouched meal of free-range roast chicken, blanched green beans, and garlic mashed potatoes. Most everyone else's plate was empty, the *A*, *Y*, and *C* initials—for Annapolis Yacht Club—now visible on the bone-white china. But Brynn couldn't bring herself to take a single bite.

The girl next to her, whose name tag read FRANCESCA CLARK, dropped her napkin to the floor and bumped against Brynn's elbow as she scrambled to pick it up. "I'm so sorry," she said emphatically, her gray eyes widening.

Brynn gave her a weak, distracted smile. "It's okay." Tension was high tonight. Her table was full of students like her, kids whose weekends were spent at chemistry fairs and Knowledge Bowl competitions, whose summers consisted of Ivy League science camps and fancy internships, and they all were working out their jitters in different ways. Two seats away, Vishal Singh, whom Brynn had sat next to at several award ceremonies just like this one, was in a cranky argument about quarks with the guy next to him, whose name tag read ADAM ROSE. Across the table, Faith Huffington, by Brynn's estimation a decent contender to win the Dove, chewed on her nails so rabidly Brynn wouldn't have been surprised if she bit one clean off. And Francesca Clark, a girl unfamiliar to Brynn, with skin so bloodless she seemed almost translucent, was smoothing her cloth napkin over her lap again and again—clearly a nervous tic.

Brynn gazed at the other guests in the room. There were her mother, pharmaceutical scientist Dr. Celeste Caldwell, and her father, Edward Caldwell, at a table toward the back. Brynn's boyfriend, Dex Kinsley, sat with her family, dutifully making conversation with her dad. Then Brynn's gaze swung to the head table, closest to the podium. There sat the judges: Michael Quigley, billionaire, who gave major endowments to brilliant kids so that they could launch innovative new apps. George Costas, a luminary in the field of artificial intelligence. Maryam Chiani, who had invented an aeronautics-grade hoverboard that was being developed by the military. And, finally, Senator Robert Merriweather—a former Navy SEAL and a proponent of tightened national security and STEM programs. Senator Merriweather was one of those politicians who brazenly shared his opinion on any cable news network or radio program that gave him an audience, and he was incredibly well-known wherever he went. Brynn didn't always agree with his ideas, but the thought of sharing the stage with such a powerful personality made her stomach wobble like the chocolate pudding she'd spied on the dessert tray.

She felt a tap on her arm. "What's that?" murmured a voice.

Francesca Clark, her table-mate, was staring at a folded piece of paper in Brynn's lap. Brynn had been creasing it back and forth instead of eating.

"Um, my speech," Brynn admitted. "In case I win."

Francesca's snow-white skin paled even further. "We were supposed to write a speech?"

Vishal broke from his argument and laughed cruelly. "Uh, yeah. How could you not know that?"

A few other kids at the table tittered. Francesca pressed her lips together tightly as if she might cry. She had frizzy, fly-away hair and delicately small ears, and she wore an ill-fitting floral dress that bunched at the shoulders and came down past her knees. She looked like the kind of girl who walked out of restrooms with toilet paper on her shoe. Despite this being an übercompetitive moment, Brynn felt the urge to put her hand comfortingly on the girl's shoulder.

But then Senator Merriweather stood and strode onto the stage, and everyone at the table snapped to attention. When the senator, who was fortyish with a head of salt-and-pepper hair and a body that rivaled any muscular eighteen-year-old's, tapped the microphone, a hush fell over the crowd. Faith Huffington softly whistled.

"Thank you for coming," the senator said. Brynn's stomach flipped at hearing his familiar husky tone. "I am honored to present tonight's National Dove Award for the student who has excelled in the field of chemical engineering. As we all know, chemical engineering will become an even more powerful science in the coming years, especially in the war on global terrorism." He looked around commandingly at the audience. "As judges, we've had to parse through a very impressive field of applicants."

Brynn glanced around nervously. Impressive field of applicants was right—everyone had a formidable résumé, including Brynn. She thought about the methane-powered vehicle she'd helped build freshman year and the fact that she'd won the national ChemE Jeopardy championship as a sophomore. Two summers ago she and a team at Brown University had created a type of foam that could filter contaminated water and make it drinkable again. Brynn had a quick, agile mind that excelled at science, just like her mother. But was it enough?

It has to be, she thought. She needed this win, badly. She'd had a little blip last year, getting too wrapped up in a relationship and dropping the ball in school. The Dove would prove she was back on track.

"And now, for the winner of this year's Dove." Senator Merriweather opened an envelope. "I am proud to announce that it goes to . . ."

Brynn's heart pounded. She shut her eyes and began to repeat mnemonic tricks she'd learned to memorize scientific facts: *Dear King Philip Come Over For Good Spaghetti* for the Linnaean taxonomy in biology. *Sir Can Rig a VCR, Pal* for the brightest stars in the sky. They served as distractions from her single thundering wish: *Please, please, please pick me.*

"Francesca Clark!"

For a moment, all Brynn could hear was fuzzy feedback ringing in her ears. Francesca was so stunned she didn't close her mouth, showing off the bite of potatoes on her tongue. Everyone at the table glared at her, but people at other tables began to clap dutifully. Finally, Brynn poked Francesca's arm. "Hey," she whispered hoarsely. *"You won."*

Francesca snapped to life. She looked panicked. "B-But I don't have anything to say!"

Brynn stared at the frazzled girl. Even though Francesca

was a hot mess, she was clearly a force to be reckoned with, like one of those moths in the Amazon that looked harmless but actually could dispel a deadly poison. After all, she'd been talented enough, smart enough, to beat Brynn out for the Dove.

"Francesca Clark?" The senator squinted into the bright lights. "Are you here?"

Francesca's lip quivered. Her gaze was still locked on Brynn. Groaning, Brynn shoved the speech that had taken her three days to perfect into the girl's small, trembling hands. Francesca stared at the unexpected gift, her eyes boggling. Brynn nudged her head toward the stage. "Don't forget to thank *your* teachers and parents, not mine. Now go."

Francesca stood awkwardly, bumping her knee against the bottom of the table. All the drinking glasses wobbled. Vishal glared at Brynn. "Why'd you do *that?*"

Brynn glared back. "Because I'm not an asshole."

Once Francesca made it to the stage, the senator handed her a Dove statue and a huge bouquet of bloodred roses. Brynn dared to peek back at her parents. Her mother was politely clapping, but her father caught Brynn's eye. He shrugged as if to say, *You win some, you lose some.* But they had to be disappointed.

It's because of my blip, she thought. Of course that was why she'd lost. She'd applied for the Dove a full year ago, when she did have the prize in the bag. But the judges considered years' worth of work, and the end of the last school year and this summer had been a game changer for her. They had cost her everything.

A sob rose in her throat. She felt so blindsided...and so foolish. She quickly stood. She needed some air.

Seemingly sensing Brynn's discomfort, Dex stood, too. As Francesca began her acceptance speech—*Brynn's* acceptance speech—Brynn made her way toward the side doors, and Dex followed. "I'd like to begin with a quote by Robert Oppenheimer...," Francesca read from Brynn's notes, her voice surprisingly steady and certain. Brynn shut her eyes, her ache palpable. It had taken her ages to find that quote.

Just before edging out the door, Brynn noticed a familiar face and turned. There, sitting at one of the back tables, half hidden in the shadows, was her old friend Lexi Gates. But Lexi wasn't watching Francesca read Brynn's speech. Her gaze was on Brynn, and her expression was unreadable. Brynn's stomach did a flip. Why was *she* here?

"Come on." Dex grabbed her hand and pulled open the side exit door. Brynn hurried into the cold. It would be good to get out of that room. There was no need to hear the rest of Francesca's speech, after all. She already knew it by heart.

BRYNN AND DEX walked across the little bridge that connected the city of Annapolis to the borough of Eastport. She could smell the salty, briny Chesapeake beneath them. The sun had just set, creating a hazy, luminous glow on the horizon. But Brynn didn't feel very luminous right then. She tightened her grip around Dex's fingers and wiped her leaky eyes.

"It sucks," Dex grumbled as a group of Naval Academy midshipmen, dressed in their crisp white uniforms, marched past. "You were robbed."

Brynn sighed heavily. "No, I wasn't. I mean, when I was a kid, I won every science fair and contest I entered. It was so . . . easy. But everything's more competitive now. I have to bring my A game every day. And last year definitely didn't help."

"Don't beat yourself up about last year." Dex snaked an arm around her waist as they stepped off the bridge and onto the sidewalk, which was messy with a combination of slush and mud. "You're brilliant. And two years from now, you'll be at some amazing college, and losing the Dove won't even matter."

"The Dove would have looked great on a scholarship application, though." Brynn blew out a breath. "My parents definitely can't pay for a top-tier school out of pocket."

Dex gave her an impish smile. "What about after Cortexia's launch?"

Brynn licked her lips. Maybe that was true. Her mom had just patented a medication called Cortexia that promised to eliminate the symptoms of post-traumatic stress disorder. The medication's public launch was in less than two weeks, and the press was going bananas about it. Her mother had been tight-lipped about the financial repercussions of the patent, but didn't someone who created something amazing and life-changing deserve to make a profit?

They stopped under a streetlight, and Dex pulled Brynn to him and nestled her close. He was so tall, and she was barely five feet, so when they snuggled, her ear was close to his chest, and she could hear his heartbeat. She breathed deeply. By some delightful biochemical twist of fate, Dex's skin just naturally smelled like freshly baked bread.

"Look," he said, leaning back so he could look her in the eye. "You're still at the top of the class. You still have a college application that makes mine look like something a first grader threw together. And what about that program at Brown this summer? You should apply. *That* will go a long way toward MIT."

"That Brown program is awfully expensive," Brynn said with uncertainty. She shoved her hands into the pockets of her wool coat, suddenly feeling exhausted. "Maybe I'm blowing this out of proportion."

"Maybe." A chilly wind kicked up, and Dex cupped his hands over Brynn's to warm them. "Try to appreciate what you have, not what you don't. It can change so quickly."

With a pang, Brynn realized what Dex meant. She thought of the family portrait that hung on the wall in his foyer. Dex stood on the left with his mother's arm around him. Mr. Kinsley stood tall and proud next to Dex's brother, Marc, regal in his army uniform. How happy they all looked.

Like nothing bad would ever befall them. The photo had been taken shortly before Marc went to Afghanistan. After that, life had thrown them a curveball... and not a very good one.

Dex was frowning now, probably thinking about it, too.

Brynn's heart sank. It was petty to whine about losing the Dove. She did need to keep things in perspective. "I'm an idiot. I've been so selfish."

Dex waved her comment away. "Nah. You're disappointed. It's only human."

They fell into an awkward silence all the same. Brynn shut her eyes, wishing she could just take a big eraser to this day and wipe it clean. More than that, she wished she knew some magic words that would break Dex from his endless sadness over his brother. Whenever he thought about Marc's death, he seemed to fold into a tight, origami version of himself, and sometimes he didn't break out of the mood for hours.

"What are you drawing?" Dex asked suddenly.

Brynn glanced down. Unconsciously, she'd traced an octagonal shape into the muddy slush with the point of her heel. She knocked the gunk off her shoe. "Nothing," she said absently. The shape reminded her of something... but then the wisp of a memory floated out of her mind.

Experimentally, she slipped her hand back into Dex's. To her relief, he squeezed it. "Are you doing better?" she asked.

"Yeah," he answered. "You?"

Brynn nodded, but she still felt teary-eyed. "I just want to make a difference in the world," she said softly. "I want to make my mark—like my mom. But I know that takes hard work. Never taking your eyes off the prize."

"You will make your mark. I know it." He sniffed. "Besides, I don't know why you wanted to accept an award from Senator Merriweather, anyway." He made a face.

"You and my mom both. She's always talking about how he's a right-wing nut."

"I heard him say in a speech that he thinks it should be a law that every American carry a weapon because we have no idea where the terrorists are hiding." He scoffed. "The last thing we need is more people like *that*."

Brynn waved him away. "Isn't half of what everyone says on TV taken out of context? You have to admit he's kind of dazzling in person."

"Yeah, well." Dex whipped out his phone and tapped an app, and to Brynn's surprise, an image of a bouquet of flowers appeared on the screen. "Who would you rather get flowers from? That Merriweather tool or me?"

Brynn giggled. "You, obviously." She pretended to take the flowers, then pretended to accept an imaginary Dove from Dex's outstretched arms. At his encouragement, she even rattled off the first few lines of her speech. Dex proclaimed she delivered it with much more aplomb than Francesca. Brynn appreciated him trying to make her feel better despite his pain. He was always so boundlessly kind. It was one of the reasons she'd fallen for him.

Only when she heard a motor rev did she turn. A gray Toyota Corolla with tinted windows was parked on a side street nearby. Its parking lights were on, and though Brynn couldn't see inside, it felt like the driver was watching her. Her skin prickled. She nervously cleared her throat.

"What's wrong?" Dex asked.

"Was that car parked there a few minutes ago?"

He squinted. "I have no idea. Why does it matter?"

Her gaze remained on the car. All of a sudden, her throat felt tight. Her hands flew to her windpipe, and she gasped for air. In her mind, she saw herself huddling in a dark, cramped space, a memory she couldn't remember actually experiencing. She so badly wanted to scream, but she didn't have the strength to do so.

Breathe, she told herself. *You're okay.* A few months ago, she'd fallen into a deep depression, and many of her days had been spent in a state of trapped helplessness. Occasionally, a panic attack would still rear its ugly head, and she had to remind herself that she'd beat the disease. She'd climbed out of the dark, slippery hole by taking an SSRI for a while, which recalibrated her brain chemistry.

"Brynn. *Brynn.* What is it?"

She opened her eyes again. Dex was looking at her with concern. Her tongue felt coated with flour as she tried to speak. "It's nothing," she whispered. "I'm okay." She took huge breaths, imagining the panic melting into a puddle.

"Are you sure?"

The Corolla pulled out of the parking spot and headed down the street. Taking a shaky breath, Brynn grabbed Dex's hand and kissed his gorgeous, sensitive, caring face.

"I'm sure," she said, and it was true. Her heart was already slowing to its normal rhythm. Whatever had happened had thankfully passed. The more Brynn thought about it, the more she was sure it was just a by-product of all the stress she'd felt leading up to the Dove Award. But all at once she didn't really care that she'd lost. She might not have captured tonight's prize, but she had something better.

She had Dex.

TWO

ELEVEN DAYS TO LAUNCH

On Monday morning, as Brynn shuffled down to breakfast in her MIT Research Science Institute camp T-shirt, plaid pajama pants, and slippers that bore the frazzled, wild-haired likeness of Albert Einstein on the toes, she came upon her parents. Her mother sat in the breakfast nook with Martin, her assistant at the lab. Martin was making notes on a clipboard. His skin had a greasy sheen, and his hair was flattened to the left side of his head. He was also wearing two different-colored socks. Brynn didn't know if it was because he was exhausted or because he was just absentminded. Brynn's father stood at the island eating a lox-slathered raisin bagel, a flavor combination Brynn had never understood.

"Hey, sweetie," her parents said in unison as she entered, their smiles holding a hint of concern. Brynn looked away and distracted herself by stroking Marley, the family's cat, who liked to lurk around the kitchen in the hope of getting a dish of milk. Brynn could tell they wanted to discuss how she felt about losing the Dove, but she would rather have let it go. She didn't like to dwell on the past.

Martin tapped his clipboard to get her mom's attention. "Okay, so you have an interview with the *Washington Post* at ten this morning, and then at ten thirty, some people from the FDA have arranged to meet at the office."

Brynn's mother tucked a piece of dirty-blond hair behind her ear. "But there's no way I'm going to be finished with the interview by ten thirty."

"Oh." Martin's hand flailed to his chin, almost knocking over his glass of orange juice. "I didn't think of that."

Brynn's father was still in his blue flannel pajamas; the National Symphony Orchestra, for which he played second-chair oboe, was off for the season, and he didn't have to go in for rehearsals until the afternoon. He set down his bagel and ran his hand over his thinning hair. "Celeste, it might be worth it to hire a personal assistant to handle this stuff instead of burdening Martin. I'm sure he'd rather be doing his *normal* work."

Martin looked grateful. "I agree. I don't know what I'm doing at *all*."

Dr. Caldwell bit the end of her pen. Her lips looked

chapped. "But Ed, we don't have the money for that right now."

"Right *now* we don't, but I'm sure we could put a little on credit, don't you think? This seems awfully important."

Dr. Caldwell peered at Martin's clipboard, and Brynn did too, over her shoulder. The page on top was a calendar where Martin had penned in countless interviews, talks, and meetings.

"I can handle it," Brynn's mom said, making the same pained face she'd made when the mechanic had told her that her ancient Volvo needed a brand-new engine. Brynn knew she was balking because she hated spending money on useless things. Half the time, money didn't even enter into her consciousness. And inventing Cortexia wasn't about the vast amount of cash that might come with it. Her mother's only goal was to help people who were suffering. It was why she'd invited quite a few of the soldiers who were part of the clinical trials to family dinners—and to the launch event.

Brynn's mom leaned back in her chair. "Besides, a personal assistant won't help me get through so many interviews—I have to do that all on my own." She glanced worriedly at Brynn's father. "It's so daunting. I'm so afraid my mind is going to go blank."

Edward Caldwell walked over and massaged her shoulders with his long, sinuous musician's fingers. "It can't be any different than presenting your research at a conference.

Or pretend you're talking to Brynn and me over dinner. Tell the interviewer about your early work. How your experiments with brain mapping led to some exploratory thinking about how we could possibly *alter* the brain's makeup—and how it stores memories."

"Yes, yes, that's good." Dr. Caldwell grabbed the clipboard from Martin and scribbled notes on it. "And with the help of Dr. Alfred Lowell, my lab partner, we patented a chemical that acted on the brain safely and quickly, rerouting specific neurological pathways to sort of . . . detour around certain memories. It was a really exciting time."

Understatement. When it was being developed, Brynn's mother gave Brynn and her dad the play-by-play of Cortexia's journey. Her team used rats in the early experiments. First, they dangled a large stuffed happy face in front of the rats, then administered an electric shock. The team mapped the brain activity that happened as the rats got the shock . . . and the activity that occurred every time the rats saw the happy face thereafter, even if a shock wasn't given. Not surprisingly, as time went on, the rats panicked whenever the face came into view. It was a Pavlovian response, and they became skittish. Paranoid. They had the rat version of PTSD.

Enter the chemical compound named Cortexia. Using the new serum Brynn's mother spent years perfecting, her team injected the affected rodents, which put them into a suggestive state, where their feelings and emotions and memories could be altered more easily. Immediately, a trained animal psychologist began to "rewire" the trigger memories, showing the rats the happy face while showering them with praise and treats. They rewired the memories. Lessened their trauma. Then came the moment of truth: subjecting the rats to their traumatic memories *without* a Cortexia injection. Had their experiments worked? Could memories change?

One day, Brynn's mom came home from the lab in such a daze she pulled out a chair for herself and then sat down in a totally different spot, plopping to the floor. "We put the happy face in front of the rats today, and they didn't panic. We watched their brain activity on the monitor, but there were no effects. They're fine. They're *cured.*" She trembled with excitement. "Anyone who's been through anything terrible can benefit from this. It will change the world."

Brynn's father whooped. "Damn right it will." To celebrate, they'd gone out for crab cakes. At the cheap place—because a researcher's salary and the pittance a symphony musician made didn't allow them fancy dinners. But that night, to Brynn, the meal tasted like it cost a million bucks.

Brynn had been in fifth grade at the time of the Great Rat Experiments, and she had assumed Cortexia would be in the pharmacy the following year. "No," her mother had corrected her. "Cortexia will have to go through many, many trials before people can use it as a treatment. People aren't rats. Their problems are much more emotionally complicated, and obviously there's a psychotherapeutic piece to the puzzle, too—it's the doctor who changes the memories. Cortexia merely allows someone's mind to open to that change. So we still have lots of testing to do."

Or so they had thought. Retelling it in their kitchen now, Dr. Caldwell picked up the story, going into full-on rehearsal mode. Her gray-blue eyes were bright. "The FDA, influential government programs, lobbyists, high military officials, and, of course, BioXin, saw the promise in the treatment. No one wanted to wait years to approve this thing—people needed help *now*. Cortexia was fast-tracked through the trial stages. Tons of people voluntarily signed up for testing, though we could only take a select few who we thoroughly screened beforehand. We worked around the clock, got a lot of promising psychotherapists on board, and, with their help, got very promising results. Soldiers who were in the throes of depression could finally function again. Live normal lives. Have families. Even be happy." Dr. Caldwell smiled dreamily. "Six years later, the drug is ready to be rolled out for the general public. So many people need this medication. It's going to save so many lives."

"Bravo!" Brynn's father applauded. "That's perfect." He smothered her in a hug. "Everyone is going to love it—and love *you*."

Brynn hid a grateful smile. Thank God her parents were back to normal. Mere months ago, they were barely speaking. When Brynn came into a room, the air crackled with the tension of a fight she'd just missed. She heard slamming doors and heated whispers. When her mother had answered her father's calls, she spoke in clipped, one-word sentences, and no longer signed off with an "I love you" or a smoochy-kiss sound.

Are they just stressed? she'd written in her journal. *Or are they worried about me? They probably hate me, actually. Just like Jacob does.*

Jacob. He was Brynn's ex; he'd broken up with her at the same time her parents' fights began. Jacob was sexy. Sultry. Wickedly smart. The kind of guy you couldn't help falling in love with. Gorgeous, too. But when Brynn tried to picture him in her mind these days, she could only see his searing gaze and permanent sneer. It was probably better to remember him that way, considering how badly everything had ended.

Brynn had met him while touring the Johns Hopkins campus last March; his family lived in Annapolis, too, but he went to a different school on the other side of town. After a series of deep-thoughts texts and flirty Snapchats, she and Jacob became one of those couples joined at the hip. *You make me the best me I can be,* Jacob always said to her. *And I want to make you the best you. Will you let me?*

Of course Brynn wanted to let him. It entranced her that Jacob wanted to polish her to a shine. It was only afterward, when she looked back, that she realized that what first seemed like gentle encouragement was actually kind of . . . controlling.

It had happened so gradually that Brynn hadn't even realized. But now, when she looked through old texts and emails, she realized how patronizing and prescriptive Jacob had been. When he wrote an email about how he didn't like a particular short pink skirt she'd worn on a date because it would give guys the wrong idea, Brynn gave the skirt to Chloe, a girl in her French class. Another email was about how he'd rather she didn't take pottery with Mr. Baskin, an attractive teacher in his twenties. *He seems like the kind of dude who checks out girls in the hall.* Brynn had no clue what he meant—Jacob was judging the guy from a random picture on the school's Facebook page. Mr. Baskin wasn't like that in real life. But it wasn't a coincidence that Brynn had switched to Ms. Leiber's class afterward.

Only later did she realize how many times she'd replied *I'm sorry,* even when all she'd done was miss one of his calls because she was hanging out with Lexi. Jacob had never met Lexi—which seemed intentional, because Brynn had tried to get them together plenty of times. He disliked everyone in her life who directed her attention away from him, though he twisted even that into something earnest and sweet: He said he loved her so much that he wanted her all to himself. What girl wouldn't be flattered by that?

By the end of the school year, Brynn had mostly dropped her friends and was seeing Jacob all the time. And she was changing—staying out after curfew, sneaking into DC when she was supposed to be in school, ditching dinners with her parents so she and Jacob could go to R-rated movies. She ended the school year with a B-plus average, and she'd never gotten less than an A before. It had felt worth it, though—Jacob had become her everything. He'd turned into the only thing that mattered. Brynn trusted he would be with her, always.

Until he wasn't. Midsummer, Jacob stopped calling. When he hadn't texted for days, she sent email after worried email. Jacob finally replied to say he'd decided to enroll in the University of Colorado a year early; he'd already left for summer classes. Brynn had been stunned. She wasn't even worth saying good-bye to. She didn't matter to him at all.

The rest of that summer, she hid under the covers, wallowing in worthlessness. It was a weird, blurry, shadowy state. Her dreams had blended with reality, and vice versa. Afterward, she read that people in a deep depression often have trouble sorting each day from the next. It scared her that her brain could actually shut down, but that's exactly what it did.

When the first day of school arrived, she had to drag herself to class. Kids stared; she'd lost weight since June. The first day at ChemE Jeopardy practice, Brynn, the returning champion, didn't answer a single question, her brain too sluggish to beat the buzzer. The phone rang after the second day of school, and she heard her mother talking in hushed tones, whispering Brynn's name, saying they'd have a talk with her.

Brynn didn't know who'd called, nor did she remember the follow-up talk. Her mom must have been smooth, though, because as far as Brynn knew, there were no further phone calls to their house. Of course, that also might have been because Brynn's doctor put her on an SSRI for depression; after a few weeks, the fog lifted. Gradually, the world felt clearer. Brynn's sleep was deeper and more restful. She no longer curled up in a scared ball in the shower—and she was once again *taking* showers. Brynn's parents went back to being the loving, stable couple she'd always known, too, which made Brynn wonder if her troubles had broken them apart, and her healing was bonding them back together.

Every morning that Brynn took a pill, she felt crisper, steadier, more like herself. School made sense again. She aced the first few tests of the year and was elated, an emotion she hadn't felt in a long time. Cheesy as it was, she saw herself as a poster girl for an antidepressant commercial, the smiling "After" person who rowed a boat on a lake and ran through a field with a balloon. Her doctor said she was doing so well on the medication that she could ease off it if she wanted, little by little. Though Brynn had been afraid to try at first—what if the symptoms came back?—she dutifully started cutting the pills in half, then in quarters. Just recently, she'd gone off them completely.

And then, in physics, Brynn started talking to Dex Kinsley, a new kid at Eastport High that year. Dex was a great cross-country runner and had quirky taste in movies, and they discovered they both loved Monty Python, which Jacob used to make fun of her for watching. He was a good listener, and soon Brynn found herself spilling her guts about Jacob and their breakup, her depression, and her parents' fights. It was so easy to talk to Dex—like she'd known him forever. In telling Dex her stories, Brynn understood what a jerk Jacob had been. No guy should make you feel worthless. Slowly, she began to realize again that she *was* worth something... and that she had the right to say no... *and* that she had the right to wear short skirts and take pottery from the cute male pottery teacher anytime she damn well pleased.

She felt back on track. Maybe ready for a new relationship, even—though she vowed to get involved with Dex with her eyes wide open. It didn't hurt that he was gorgeous— and extremely sexy and smart—but she was doing things on *her* terms this time. It was Brynn who'd made the first move, in fact, once she felt ready. She smiled at the memory.

Her mother looked up and noticed Brynn by the kitchen island. "What are you doing? You're going to be late."

Brynn stared down at the uneaten piece of toast in her hands. "On it," she said, springing back to her room to get ready for school.

Twitter had automatically refreshed on her computer screen, and Brynn noticed that Francesca Clark had sent her a private message. *Thank you again!* she gushed, attaching a picture of herself and the senator. Brynn smiled sadly, then clicked away from the window.

She flung open her closet, revealing a jumble of plaid shirts, casual dresses, and ripped jeans. At the very back, she noticed a hot-pink hoodie. Lexi had left it behind almost a year before, when they were still tight. She'd never come to retrieve it.

Lexi. Brynn felt as unsettled about her old friend as she did about Jacob. Why had she been at the Dove ceremony? Had she come to support Brynn, like old times? Should Brynn text her? But she hadn't spoken to Lexi in months. . . . What would she even say?

Beep.

A text appeared on Brynn's phone. At first, she thought it might *be* from Lexi—they used to claim they could read each other's minds, often calling each other out of the blue at the very same time to talk about the very same thing. But this text was from a phone number that was all ones and zeros. It didn't look like a real phone number at all.

Are you ready? It's almost time. Eleven more days.

On an impulse, she typed back, *Ready for what?*

You know.

Uh, no I don't. Sorry.

Brynn tossed the phone on the bed, but it beeped once more. *You know me. And I know you. I know everything you've done. So be ready. Or else.*

Brynn stepped back as though the phone had burst into flames. Everything she'd done? That sounded so ... ominous.

Someone's just pranking you, she told herself.

An engine roared. Brynn turned toward the sound. Her bedroom curtains fluttered in the breeze. A chill snaked up Brynn's spine. *She* hadn't opened that window. . . .

She rushed over to look outside. A car peeled away from her curb, nearly squashing a squirrel running across the street. Black smoke rose from the exhaust pipe, but even so, Brynn was able to get a good look at the vehicle as it disappeared. Her heart plummeted to her shoes, and once again, she felt her throat constrict. She dropped to the ground as though suddenly chopped off at the knees. Here came the feeling of small, tight, terrifying confinement. Here came her panic. Here came her frightened tears. *No,* she told herself, battling against it all. *You're fine, you're fine.* But the attack whooshed through her regardless.

The car was a gray Toyota Corolla.

THREE

A few hours later, Brynn sat at a lab table in her AP Physics C classroom at Eastport High. The heater was on overdrive to combat the suddenly bitter cold, and the air felt stuffy and thick in the cramped space. The walls were overloaded with hyperstimulating posters: close-ups of atoms colliding, a fluorescent chart of the principles of motion and mass, a colorful photograph of balls on a pool table ricocheting in all sorts of directions to illustrate kinematics. Her teacher, Mr. Chang, had a thing about not erasing the blackboard, so every equation they'd worked on since the beginning of the year was still up there. Now, in mid-November, whenever Mr. Chang had to illustrate a new formula, he had to squeeze it in at the very bottom of the board, where it was almost impossible to see.

"Let's continue with our reports," Mr. Chang boomed after he concluded a rambling tangent about Einstein's personal life while at Princeton. "Who's up?" He consulted his list and smiled. "Aha. Miss Brynn Caldwell."

The whole class, some of whom had been at the Dove awards, swiveled around and watched silently as Brynn stood, gathered her notes, and walked to the front of the room. Sienna Mayview and Colleen Carter, her good friends pre-Jacob, gave her small smiles. Dex grinned broadly and gave her a thumbs-up.

The only person who wasn't paying attention was Lexi. She sat alone at the back table, her long reddish-brown hair a dark sheet around her face. Brynn tried to catch Lexi's eye, but her ex-friend wouldn't look up.

Brynn got to the front of the classroom and smiled at Mr. Chang. Understanding that his students were smarter than he was, Mr. Chang had given everyone a free range of topics to report on—they just had to be physics related. Most kids chose either übercomplex topics, in the hope of confounding their classmates, or else stuff seen on *MythBusters*. Brynn looked down at her notebook. She usually went the smartest-girl-in-the-room route, but today she was on the *MythBusters* path. It was a topic she'd chosen at the beginning of the school year, when she'd still been mentally checked out.

Was that when the gray car had started following her?

Stop thinking about that car, Brynn thought sharply. *No one is following you.*

But what about those texts? What was it "almost time" for? Why did she keep freaking out whenever she saw a Corolla? Was she having a mental breakdown?

"Brynn?" Mr. Chang looked at her from his desk. Brynn stared out at the sea of faces and smiled. She had this. Right?

She took a deep breath. "Okay, so you know how you're watching an action movie, and all of a sudden, a bomb explodes?" She was desperate to ditch the wiggle in her voice. "And then the main characters jump to their feet and start running really fast and manage to outrun the explosion? It's amazing. And it makes for a great Hollywood moment. But can you really outrun a bomb? I'm here to prove to you that . . . no. Even Usain Bolt cannot outrun a bomb. And here's why."

She pulled out the poster-board chart she'd made of four types of bombs: a pipe bomb in a backpack, a fifty-pound briefcase bomb, a thousand-pound device in a van, and a huge bomb inside a tractor trailer. The bigger and heavier the device, the farther away the US Department of Homeland Security recommended someone be to avoid major damage from the blast. In the case of the biggest device, you had to be half a mile away not to get hurt.

"But I'm sure you want more of the nitty-gritty," Brynn said. "I mean, how *does* a bomb hurt us?" She flipped to her next poster. "As we've learned, most bombs are made of atoms slamming together and creating a huge reaction. When there's a blast, it creates highly compressed air particles and a shock wave that carries energy through the air, throwing the fragmented shrapnel outward—way outward. Sometimes a half mile! And even more than that?" She tapped the last picture in her diagrams, which showed a blast in the center and arrows heading both toward and away from the blast. "The blast wind creates a vacuum. It refills itself with air, and it pulls the shrapnel back in. So you might get hit *twice*."

"Harsh." Chase Lansing, Brynn's buddy, who'd been her lab partner many a time over the years, looked impressed.

A hand shot up. Brynn was startled to see who was asking the question. "Uh, yeah?" She offered Lexi a small smile.

Lexi's glossy pink mouth was tight. "How do you know so much about bombs, anyway?"

Brynn's stomach did a swoop. "I'm . . . sorry?"

"You could have chosen anything, but you picked bombs. I'm just wondering why."

Brynn pushed a piece of hair out of her eyes. The question felt loaded . . . like Lexi was hinting at an inside joke Brynn was supposed to remember. Her brain cycled through options. Maybe it was something that had happened over the summer. Something deep in her lost memories. Sienna and Colleen looked at Lexi with puzzled expressions, too.

"What's the matter with bombs?" Dex piped up from his seat. "You think your report was any better? Thermodynamics. Snoozefest."

Mr. Chang cleared his throat. "All right, Mr. Kinsley. That's enough. And that's the point, Lexi. You guys can choose any topic you want. I think this is an interesting one—and, I might add, directly related to physics." He smiled at Brynn. "Continue."

Brynn nodded and looked at her charts, desperate to get her mojo back. But she felt destabilized. Lexi was still glaring at her.

A flash at the window captured her attention. A car idled at the curb outside. A gray Toyota. The windows were tinted, so Brynn couldn't see the driver, but it felt like whoever was in there was looking straight into the physics class through the window . . . *at her.*

Her charts fell from her hands. She could already feel the fault lines inside her beginning to rumble. *No,* she willed. She would *not* have an attack here. It was just a freaking *car.* There was nothing to worry about.

Sweat prickled on the back of her neck. Blood pounded in her ears. Her vision began to blur, and she fumbled behind her for the back of a chair, collapsing into the seat to save herself from tumbling to the floor. "Brynn?" she heard Mr. Chang say, but she couldn't answer him.

It was happening again. There she was, in what felt like

her memory, curled into the fetal position, whimpering, in a dark, airless, lonely place. *Help,* she heard herself calling. *Someone, please help!*

What was happening to her? Was she falling into a depression again? Had she gone off the meds too soon? *Help,* the voice in her head kept saying. *Help.* The word rang in her ears. It almost sounded familiar. . . .

When Brynn felt a hand on her arm, she opened her eyes and realized she'd spoken aloud. Maybe more than once.

She was on the floor, her presentation notes scattered around her. The room was silent, and everyone in class was out of their chairs, gathered in a tight circle around the podium. How much time had passed? Mr. Chang stood closest to Brynn, and Dex was right behind him. Everyone looked panicked.

"Brynn," Mr. Chang said. "Brynn, thank God. I've called the nurse."

Brynn blinked hard. The feeling had passed, and now she was just sweaty and dazed. "I don't need the nurse," she said in a small voice.

"Are you sure?" Dex looked like he might cry.

Brynn nodded and struggled to her feet. Dex and Mr. Chang took her hands to help stabilize her. Brynn wondered how slick her palms felt and how bad she smelled. "I'm fine."

Once upright, she turned to the window. The Toyota was pulling away. She studied the license plate: ALO3595. Her mind worked to commit it to memory. *AL* stood for *aluminum. O* for *oxygen.* Thirty-five was bromine's atomic weight. Ninety-five was americium's.

The bell rang, and everyone reluctantly backed away from Brynn and gathered their stuff at their desks. Mr. Chang cleared his throat awkwardly. "Uh, if you'd like, you can turn in your notes, and I can grade those."

Brynn scooped her papers off the ground. "Thank you," she mumbled. "And I'm sorry about—"

"Don't worry. But I do think you should go to the nurse. I can write an excuse for your next class."

"Really, I'm okay." Brynn tried to put her papers in order. In the margins of her last sheet of notes, she noticed a familiar doodle. It was the same octagon she'd traced after the award ceremony last night. An unidentifiable feeling of dread coursed through her. Though she wanted to keep the drawing, the page contained some notes critical to the presentation, so she smiled at Mr. Chang and handed it over.

Her limbs felt heavy as she trudged to her desk. She didn't realize Dex was standing next to her until he awkwardly coughed. She glanced at him quickly, then busied herself with shoving her books into her bag.

"What happened?" Dex's voice was uneasy.

Brynn shrugged. Her cheeks burned. "Low blood sugar, probably. I was too distracted to eat breakfast."

"It seemed like something you saw out the window scared you."

She zipped up her backpack pocket. "I saw a car. A Toyota. It looked like the same one I saw the other night, in the parking lot."

Dex frowned. "After the Dove awards?"

She nodded. "Yeah. But it's nothing." She considered mentioning the texts she got before school, but what was the point? They were probably just spam.

Dex ran his tongue over his teeth. "You seem so upset, babe."

Brynn turned her chin away so he wouldn't see her pained expression. "I just wish I hadn't collapsed in front of the whole class."

As they tramped into the hall, Cameron, one of Dex's cross-country friends, passed by, and they slapped each other a high five. Next to them stood Gianna Waites and Kristina Jansta, two girls on the cross-country team— and friends of Brynn's. Everyone said hi, but Brynn didn't feel like making small talk. She was too scattered. The group finally moved on, and Dex turned back to her. When he noticed the worried look still on Brynn's face, his expression clouded, too. "You know what else I'm concerned about, though?" he asked. "What Lexi said about your report.

Was that supposed to be a burn? And when you collapsed, she didn't even get up. She just sat at her desk, looking at her phone." He snorted. "I can't believe you guys were once friends."

She's not like that, normally, Brynn wanted to say. But who knew? Maybe Lexi *was* like that nowadays. It wasn't as if Brynn knew her anymore.

Sighing, she slung her backpack over her shoulder. "Let's get out of here. I need a do-over on today. On a *bunch* of days, actually."

"Are you sure you don't need the nurse?" Dex asked.

Maybe she should tell Dex what was going on. Maybe if she described the visions aloud, they'd no longer seem so scary. Maybe if she voiced how, over the last day, she suddenly felt mentally adrift, and oddly helpless, and emotionally volatile, he'd offer a simple explanation. But what if the simple explanation was that her depression was coming back? Or something worse, like she was going through a psychotic break? She couldn't share that with Dex. That sounded so intense. So . . . *sick*. Dex might not think she was good enough for him anymore.

Brynn bit down hard on her lip, furious that such an insecure thought had crossed her mind. It was the kind of thinking she'd wallowed in with Jacob: that she was never good enough, that she didn't matter, that if she made the tiniest mistake, he'd leave her. Jacob had made her feel guilty about *everything,* and those feelings still spilled over into her thoughts and decisions. That wasn't Dex, though. Thankfully, Jacob was her past, and Dex was her future.

So she pasted on her best no-worries smile. "Everything's just fine."

If only she felt that way for real.

FOUR

TEN DAYS TO LAUNCH

The wind whipped across Brynn's cheeks as she hurried up the hill at Arlington National Cemetery, and she pulled her duffle coat tighter around her. It was Tuesday afternoon, and the sun was low in the sky. Before her was a sea of identical gravestones, an abstract marvel against the bright green grass. Up ahead, she caught sight of Dex standing at a grave under a maple tree. His head was bent, and his lips were moving silently.

She crossed the path and stood by Dex's side. There, on the stone, in the same serious, important lettering as all the other headstones, was inscribed MARC KINSLEY, followed by the date Dex's brother was born and the date he died.

Without speaking, she squeezed Dex's hand. Brynn's

boyfriend had been visiting his brother's grave every Tuesday afternoon since Marc's death eighteen months ago, and ever since September, Brynn had come, too. If Brynn were being honest, she wasn't sure what these visits did for Dex; whenever he was here, the pain seemed like a vise around his chest. But she supposed it was part of the grieving process.

"How about you tell me what he was like?" Brynn asked softly. She knew it made Dex happy to reminisce about more innocent times. "Tell me something you haven't told me yet."

The corners of Dex's mouth jerked into a smile. "Well, okay." He took a breath. "He was amazing at *League of Legends*. Could beat my ass on *Mario Kart*. And every year on my birthday, he'd play an elaborate prank on me. At first, it was just a trick to get me to look away so he could shove a piece of cake in my face. But then he made stuff spring out of the bathroom when I opened the door, and one time he dressed up as a zombie and chased me up the stairs. Another time, he secretly stuck some peanut butter crackers in my jacket pocket, which made this goose that always hung out on our lawn come after me with a vengeance."

"A goose?" Brynn giggled. "That's classic."

Dex made a sound that was a combination of a laugh and a whimper. Brynn pretended not to notice—he hated when she called attention to his heightened emotions. "It's just that I want to *hurt* the people who did this to him," he said through his teeth.

She squeezed his hand. "I know."

"And I *can't*. I mean, unless I sign up for military service as well, and my parents are pulling out all the stops to make sure I don't."

"There are other ways to make changes. Political influence. Volunteering. Even that internship you did last summer with the NSA. Maybe if you work there someday, you can change policy. Make sure this never happens to anyone else."

Dex surreptitiously wiped his eyes. "I just keep waiting for it to get easier, you know? And it never does."

"It will someday. You have to believe that."

Their gazes returned to Marc's gravestone. Dex fiddled with his phone, its tiny speakers playing "Radioactive," Marc's favorite song. Well, his old favorite song. When he returned from Afghanistan, after receiving the Medal of Honor for bravery, Dex's brother enjoyed darker, harder music, shutting himself in his bedroom and listening to thrumming, atonal songs at deafening volume. People tried to laud Marc for the valor he'd shown in battle—he'd saved a bunch of soldiers from an enemy attack by allowing himself to get captured and briefly imprisoned. But according to Dex, whenever someone brought up the war, Marc got annoyed and left the room.

Dex had moved on to the next part of the Marc gravesite ritual: placing an Almond Joy, Marc's favorite snack, in front of the headstone. He unwrapped the candy and took a bite.

"Rest is for you, man." He placed the uneaten portion on the grass, then slung his arm around Brynn. "Thanks for coming."

"Of course," Brynn whispered.

"I wish you could have known him."

"Me, too." Brynn swallowed hard. Like Dex, she wished Marc were still here. For Dex's sake, yes, but also because Marc was the only person Brynn knew who'd suffered through depression, just like she had. She longed to talk to someone about it. Did Marc have gaps in his memories as well? Had there been days when he just couldn't get out of bed? It sounded like it, based on the stories Dex had told her. Brynn also wanted to tell him that it *could* get better. After all, she'd crawled out of her hole. If Marc had just found the right person to be around, maybe the right combination of drugs, might he have recovered, too?

Brynn had mentioned these thoughts and desires to Dex only once. He'd listened thoughtfully, but then said he wasn't sure Marc could have ever gotten better—his affliction was deeper than depression. "But you should really find a support group or something," he added, looking carefully at her. "Depression is no joke. What if you relapse?"

Brynn was considering it—the idea of relapsing made her anxious—but she hadn't yet found a group close to home.

They stood at the gravesite for a while longer, not speaking. What *was* there to say? It had been Dex who'd found

Marc's body at the bottom of the gorge near their house. There were headphones in his ears and alcohol in his system, and he had sixteen broken bones, including his neck. He'd gotten drunk and slipped, the police concluded. His death was an accident. A tragedy.

Brynn's phone beeped. Wincing at the sudden noise, she glanced at the screen. It was a text from her mother. *Can you grab dinner from Giant on your way home? I'm running late, and your dad's still in rehearsal.*

"I have to go. The long line at the grocery store awaits." She touched Dex's shoulder. "Wanna come with?"

"I'm going to stay here a little longer, then maybe go for a run." The wind blew Dex's hair across his forehead. "I need to clear my head."

"You're crazy to run in this cold." Brynn kissed his forehead, then started down the embankment toward the parking lot.

The gravel crunched under her shoes. It was starting to drizzle, and she hurried to her car to beat the oncoming rain. Halfway down the row of vehicles, her phone beeped again. Brynn glanced down, hoping her mother had changed her mind and they could just get takeout. But when she saw the puzzling series of zeroes and ones, her heart froze in her chest.

It's almost time. Are you ready?

Rain spattered on the phone's screen. Brynn immediately typed a response, her teeth clenched in anger.

You have the wrong number. Leave me alone.

Another beep came almost instantaneously, as though the sender was expecting this reply. *We can't. You know us. And we know you. We all just want the truth.*

The rain was falling harder now, pummeling her scalp and dripping into her eyes. At the end of the row of cars, brake lights flashed. Brynn looked up, then took a jolted step back. It was a gray Toyota Corolla. Her gaze flicked to the license plate. *Aluminum, oxygen . . .*

Oh God. Not *again.*

"Help!" Brynn called weakly, starting to tremble. But before she could really understand what she was seeing, she heard a *crack,* then saw only white. The next thing she knew, her cheek was hitting the wet gravel. She let out a small, pained groan, feeling water droplets pepper the exposed small of her back.

That was the last thing she remembered.

FIVE

Thu-thump. Thu-thump. Thu-thump.

Brynn opened her eyes, but all she saw was darkness. Her knees were tucked to her chin. She tried to sit up, but her head hit a carpeted roof. Wherever she was rolled and bucked around her, and outside there was a constant, lolling swish and *thump*. A trunk, she realized, smelling the vague tinge of upholstery. She was inside the gray Toyota.

"Help!" she called out, but the roar of the road swallowed her words. Her heart pounded frantically. Her body ached to move. Her legs ached from not being able to extend, and she'd lost all feeling in her left arm. She felt trapped and helpless, controlled by a nameless, faceless force. *Just like the visions,* she thought. And just like depression itself.

The car stopped abruptly, and she rolled awkwardly to the front of the trunk. The engine shut down, doors slammed, and there were footsteps. When the trunk lid lifted, Brynn squinted into the sudden, bright light. A silhouette loomed over her. Brynn strained in the glare, but she was unable to see who it was.

The figure bent down, clapped a meaty hand over her eyes, and scooped her up. Someone hurried behind her and pushed a bag over her head. Brynn thrashed and kicked, but that just earned her a sharp jab to her side. She wailed in pain, twisting in the person's arms. Whoever it was smelled like sweat and dampness and something else—cigars, maybe. Tobacco.

She heard a *beep* and then a latch releasing. A door slammed shut behind them. Her skin prickled in the sudden frigidity of air-conditioning. "Where are we going?" she screamed, clawing at empty air. "Please, please let me go!"

"Stop talking," said the person carrying her. A man. His breath was hot in her ear.

Another door opened. Crying now, Brynn felt her body being rotated and then lowered into a padded, forgiving dentist-type chair. Hands went to work securing her wrists and tying her ankles.

"Stop, please!" Brynn called out. Someone elbowed her jaw, and she cried out. Her tears were salty in her mouth.

Someone ripped the bag from her head. Another bright light assaulted Brynn, and she squinted in pain. A blurry shape was moving a few feet away from her. When the shape came closer, Brynn could make out a man's round, intense eyes, but no other features—he was wearing a surgical mask over his mouth and nose, and a white hat that covered his hair and forehead.

"What do you know?" the man demanded from under the mask. He had a smooth, slightly deep voice. "How much did you find out?"

Brynn's mouth felt dry. She tried to move her arms and legs, but it was useless—the straps that secured her were too tight. "I—I have no idea what you're talking about," she said.

The man scowled, then glanced over his shoulder. "We need to do this." His gaze returned to Brynn. He grabbed her arm roughly, surely causing a bruise. Brynn let out a scream. She heard something crash in the distance—a slam, maybe a door breaking open. She closed her eyes in fear and anticipation—of what, she didn't know.

"Miss. *Miss!*"

Her eyes popped open. She was lying on her back, not in a chair, and her arms and legs weren't shackled. An older man Brynn vaguely recognized held her wrist like he was taking her pulse. "Miss, are you okay?"

Brynn looked around. She was still in the cemetery parking lot. The man standing over her was the groundskeeper— she'd seen him plenty of times before. Dex's car was still here, and so was hers . . . but the gray Toyota's space was empty. She looked at her wrists and ankles. There were no marks from being bound. Her skin showed no signs of a growing bruise. She experimentally touched her head, anticipating a knot of pain from where she'd been struck just before they'd thrown her into the trunk. There was no ache. Her skin didn't even feel tender.

Did she imagine the whole thing?

The groundskeeper sat back on his haunches. "I think you passed out."

Brynn moved her limbs. Everything seemed to be in working order. But when she closed her eyes, she kept seeing herself lying in that dark room. *What do you know?* Tears welled in her eyes.

Someone wanted to hurt her.

She glanced at the groundskeeper, then at the hill that led to the gravestones. "Did you see anyone in the parking lot with me?" she asked the groundskeeper. "Did someone *hit* me?"

The man's lips twitched beneath his mustache. "My goodness. I don't think so."

She pointed to the empty parking space. "Did a car just leave?"

He shook his head. "There hasn't been traffic in or out of here in the last half hour."

Brynn glanced at the big metal clock at the gates. It was

4:07. Her mother had texted her at four on the dot. How could that have been only seven minutes ago? How could an assailant have thrown her into a trunk, driven her somewhere, interrogated her, and then returned her to this very spot?

The groundskeeper narrowed his eyes. "How about I call an ambulance."

Brynn took a shaky breath. All of a sudden, she needed some space. "No, I think I'm fine. Thank you."

The man looked like he didn't believe her, but he reluctantly climbed back on his four-wheeler and rode off. Brynn remained rooted to the ground, hugging her knees to her chest, barely feeling the rain on her head. Some of the gravel was disturbed from where she'd fallen. Could she have just passed out?

Crack.

Her head shot up. Dex? His car was still here. He was probably still at his brother's grave. She should go find him, shouldn't she? Tell him what had just happened?

But what *had* just happened? Why did it feel like an actual memory—but one she couldn't actually remember? Was what she'd been feeling in the past day not her depression creeping back but something . . . *else*? Something more?

Crack. There it was again. Brynn shot to her feet, her head immediately feeling woozy. There was still someone here, watching. *Listening.*

Hands trembling, she reached for her cell phone. She could call the police. Those texts alone qualified as harassment. And she could report that the car was following her around—she knew its license plate number.

But she paused before dialing, that sinking feeling swirling in her again. The man's words hovered in her mind. *What do you know?* And then the earlier text: *We know what you've done.*

She let her phone fall to her side. She didn't know what she'd done. She didn't know what she'd just seen. So maybe it wasn't a good idea to call the police quite yet. Deep down, she had a sinking feeling she wasn't totally innocent. She felt guilty.

And she had to find out why.

SIX

The sky was dark when Brynn finally got home. Chinese takeout swung from her wrists—she'd considered going to the supermarket, but walking up and down the bright, cheerful aisles as though nothing was amiss didn't seem possible, so she'd ducked into the to-go place next door instead. As she struggled through the front door with the bags of food, she heard voices in the dining room. Way more voices than usual, in fact. A golden light much brighter than their rickety chandelier's spilled into the hallway.

"Okay, we're rolling," a voice boomed. "Quiet."

The dining room table and chairs had been removed, as had the whiteboard her mother used to sketch formulas or brainstorm ideas. In their place were three upright chairs and a whole bunch of professional-looking photography lights on stands. Brynn's mother, in a blue suit and high black heels, her hair combed sleek and straight, sat next to her partner, Dr. Alfred Lowell. Lowell was older than her mother, with tufty gray hair, round wire-rimmed glasses, and a proclivity toward garish, tacky bow ties. He caught Brynn's eye and gave her a small nod. Brynn tried to nod back, but it wasn't easy. A full house was the last thing she needed right now. She set the takeout bags on the ground with a disgruntled thump.

Someone grabbed her arm, and, still on edge, she spun her head to the left.

"Shhh," her father whispered. "They're taping an interview."

Brynn raised her eyebrows and peered back into the dining room. Across from her mom and Dr. Lowell was none other than Rainer Wilson, a handsome journalist from a famous TV newsmagazine program. Normally, this would have delighted her, but after the day she'd had, she just felt annoyed.

"You should have told me," she hissed to her dad. "I would have hoped the first time I met a major journalist I'd be a little more dressed up!"

"It only came together an hour ago. Rainer Wilson had a hole in his schedule." Her dad slung his arm around Brynn's shoulders. "Do I smell General Tso's chicken? That's sweet of you, honey. There's a huge craft services spread in the kitchen, too."

Brynn wriggled away from his embrace. "Again, something that would have been useful to know *before* I waited at China Palace for food." She so could have used those thirty minutes deep under her covers, trying desperately not to think about the vision that had dominated her brain.

"Sorry for the mix-up," her father murmured.

"I mean, I'm not even *hungry*," Brynn went on, her emotions getting the best of her. All at once, she felt like she might cry. "And there was this thing that happened at the cemetery just now—"

"Honey," her dad whispered sharply, one finger to his lips. "Can we talk about this later? The interview is very important for your mom."

Brynn glowered at him. She probably wouldn't have told her dad specifics about what had happened at the cemetery, but would it kill him to listen for just a second? But no, his gaze was on the dining room. Dr. Caldwell was giving Rainer Wilson a kindly, slightly astonished smile. "Just because our drug trials were conducted over a shorter period doesn't mean we haven't done our due diligence. We did massive amounts of testing. Also, to receive the treatment, it absolutely must be given in tandem with a psychologist or psychiatrist who's been to our training programs and works extensively with PTSD patients. The talking part of the therapy is key. It's the psychologists who actually talk the patient through overcoming the traumatic memories. Cortexia just facilitates that."

Wilson raised an eyebrow. "In other words, Cortexia and its psychological component simply hypnotize people into forgetting?"

"That's not how I like to think about it," Brynn's mother said smoothly. "I would say it's about being in a state of mind where you can move past the memories that give you pain."

Brynn's problems muscled their way into her thoughts again. She wouldn't mind moving past some memories that brought *her* pain, especially from the past two days. She peeked out the front window, half expecting to see a gray car. The curb was empty. But would it stay that way?

She thought about the man's eyes, from the dream. She swore she knew those eyes. But from *where*?

She turned and started up the stairs. "Brynn?" Her father looked shocked. "Aren't you going to stay and watch the rest of this? Your mom needs your support!"

Brynn knew she was disappointing her dad, but all at once, fleeing was more important. "Not tonight," she said woodenly, and hurried away as quickly and quietly as she could.

In the upstairs hall, her phone beeped in her pocket. Dex. *I saw the groundskeeper on the way out of the cemetery. He said you seemed really dazed. Is everything okay?*

Brynn bit her lip. *Should* she tell Dex? But how could

she do that if she didn't know herself? She wanted to get a better sense of what was happening before she got into it. Was this something chemical, like depression, or was it something scarier?

Like someone was following her. Like she'd done something awful.

Fine, she texted back to him, adding an emoji blowing a kiss. *Just tired.*

She was getting so good at lying.

IN HER BEDROOM, she flopped down on her bed and stared at her reflection in the mirror. Her shoulder-length blond hair was wild around her face. Her grayish-blue eyes were wide and scared. Her face was drawn, pale. She looked like she'd just seen a ghost. Maybe *she* was the ghost.

She reached for her phone. The first thing to do was search for any information on that gray car. *Aluminum, oxygen,* she began, grateful for the mnemonic she'd created to remember the Toyota's license plate. She found a site that could reverse-check a license number, matching it with the person who'd registered the car. After she paid the fee and entered the number, the little wheel spun, but then a blank screen appeared. The plate didn't link to a vehicle. Brynn stared. How was that possible?

Slumping back on the pillow, she tapped the Facebook app on her phone. Her news feed appeared. The first item was a video of a protest march in DC against a health and beauty company that tested on animals. Things had gotten very impassioned, and several people had been grabbed by security. Brynn stared at the angry faces in the crowd, then did a double take. Was that *Lexi*? The reddish sheet of hair disappeared quickly from view. Protesting stuff *was* sort of Lexi's thing. . . .

In ninth-grade biology, Brynn's teacher had sat her at a lab table with Lexi Gates, a new girl who was different from the other honors kids Brynn had been in class with for almost her entire school experience. Lexi had shiny red-brown hair down to her waist, wore a jumble of jingling charm bracelets she'd found at an old woman's estate sale, and carried a notebook covered in sixties folk lyrics.

She blinked at Brynn from behind long, thick lashes. "Don't you think it's totally unfair that we have to dissect animals in this class?" she whispered. "I marched with PETA in DC about this last year, you know. And now I'm considering sending a petition through the school to stop dissections because they're unethical. Wanna sign?"

"But aren't dissections important for learning?" Brynn asked.

Lexi rolled her eyes. "We could do a simulation on computers and learn just as much. The school just doesn't want to invest in it; dissecting animals is cheaper."

Lexi's passion was intriguing. Brynn had never known anyone who'd challenged the system before. As the class continued, she discovered that Lexi had also taken part in protests about human rights issues in Syria, gun control, and euthanasia. It seemed like she was always at the Capitol Building, marching for something or other. She also made funny, offbeat jokes. Her doodles of the bio teacher and other kids in the class were spot-on, and Brynn adored how she was able to talk to any guy—even a hot college student at a coffee shop—without getting sweaty or nervous. One day, when they were walking home from school, Lexi confessed that her house had been robbed when she was nine. Lexi and her mother had been tied up for hours, terrified for their lives. Though the robbers didn't hurt them, they'd smashed some of the family's precious things right in front of them. It was one of the reasons Lexi fought hard whenever she thought something was unfair or unethical—because of how powerless she'd been that night. She never wanted to be powerless again.

They'd been tight friends for two solid years: sleepovers every weekend, study sessions during the week, a ridiculous stint in a tae kwon do class, long talks about boys they had crushes on over mushroom pizza and Sprite. At first, Lexi had been thrilled for Brynn when she met Jacob, eager to hear news of their Snaps to each other, hanging on Brynn's every word about their first date. When Brynn canceled plans because Jacob wanted to see her alone, Lexi looked disappointed . . . but was still supportive. When Brynn spent an entire weekend at Lexi's family's mountain cabin texting

Jacob *I miss you* messages, Lexi got a little testy. But the straw that broke the camel's back came when Lexi offered Brynn a vape off her brother's e-cigarette. Though Brynn had tried it before, this time she refused. "Jacob says those things are a zillion times more poisonous than regular cigarettes. He doesn't get why anyone would do that to their body."

Lexi stiffened. "You know, I don't care what Jacob thinks."

Brynn felt hurt. "He's just trying to look out for us."

"Maybe for once it could just be you and me, without bringing Jacob into the conversation," Lexi snapped. "You know, I wouldn't believe he exists, the way you keep him from me. The only way I know he's real is by how he's brainwashed you."

"What?" Brynn had stared at her, and her friend had turned away, dropping the e-cigarette to the ground and running out of the room.

Beep.

Another text. Brynn clicked the messaging app, figuring Dex had written again. Instead, she saw the now-familiar jumble of numbers. Her heart started to race.

Please don't push us away. You're one *of us.*

One of them? That was impossible. Brynn gripped her phone. *I want nothing to do with you trolls, whoever you are.*

Another beep, immediately. *We only have ten more days.*

And you know you're one of us, if you dig deep. If you don't believe it, check the blue flash drive in your desk drawer.

Ten more days? Was Brynn supposed to know what that meant? And she didn't own a blue flash drive. How did this person know the contents of her desk drawer, anyway? She glanced around the room nervously. Had someone gotten in here besides her family? Was there a camera stashed somewhere, watching her at this very moment?

She gripped her phone, ready to reply. *Don't,* a voice in her head said. *Maybe they want you to respond. They want you to get scared. They're like terrorists, feeding off your fear.*

Irritated, she pitched her phone facedown onto the mattress. Picked up a *National Geographic* from the bedside stand. Flipped to an article about evolutionary principles in the Galapagos and tried to read. Her eyes blurred. Her heart thudded. Groaning, she stood and eyed her desk. Okay, so she'd just *check* the drawer. It couldn't hurt.

The surface of her desk was littered with notebooks, loose papers, empty water bottles, gift cards she hadn't gotten around to using, magazines, half-finished science projects, and two past-their-prime iPhones whose photos she kept meaning to upload onto her computer. Slowly, she sat down at her desk and pulled open the top drawer. Inside were paper clips, a bunch of USB cords, little tickets from a school raffle ages ago. But sitting on top of all those things, plain as day, was a blue flash drive.

Brynn shot away from the drawer as though it had burst into flames.

She eyed her bedroom door. It seemed impossible that a stranger could have broken into her house—her family had a security system that her mother armed every day before work. So had her mom put this in here? Her dad? Dr. Lowell? Her mother's assistant, Martin? But . . . *why?*

Downstairs, her mother laughed, her ringing voice joyful and pure. Brynn's stomach turned over. She should be downstairs, listening to this important interview. This was the highlight of her family's life, and an Internet bully was ruining that. But she stayed where she was. Her eyes were locked on the drive in the drawer.

Taking a deep breath, she grabbed the drive, inserted it into her computer, and waited. A folder appeared on the desktop. Brynn studied the thumbnailed files inside. One was a PowerPoint presentation she'd done on neurotransmitters last year. Another was a scan of a self-portrait she'd drawn in art class last spring. There were English reports, an outline for a history paper, and several drafts of an essay for her MIT application, even though she still had another year to apply.

She sat back dizzily. Okay. No big deal. These were her assignments. She must own a blue flash drive after all. Then her gaze dropped to the last of the files on the screen. There was a folder called ACL. The acronym didn't ring any bells. She clicked on the folder, and three files appeared. One was in Word, another looked like some sort of blueprint, and the third was a scan.

There was a creak behind her, and she jumped up, her heart leaping into her throat. Marley slunk around her open door, purring loudly. Brynn cradled him in her arms and shut the door with her foot. She had an urge, suddenly, to prevent anyone from seeing what she was looking at on the screen.

Settling back into her chair, she clicked on the Word file. An entire page was filled with long strings of numbers separated by dots. IP addresses? She typed a few into the computer; some led to computers close by, one was for inner-city DC, another from northern New Jersey. Which rang no bells.

She opened the blueprint, but it made no sense, either— it showed a generic building with little squares for rooms, demarcated lines for stairwells, and a big atrium in the center. Various exits were circled with blue pen, but there was no explanation why. Brynn chewed on her thumbnail. Where was this place? Why was a map of it on her drive?

Marley kneaded Brynn's thighs with his soft paws. She absently stroked his head. The last file was a scan full of notes in her handwriting. Frowning, Brynn tried to digest the words. There were drawings of chemical compounds and bonds. Formulas for force, pressure, and decomposition. Her mind was too addled to process what they meant, but she knew they had nothing to do with a school assignment.

So when had she written these? And for what? Her gaze drifted to the bottom of the page. There, again in her small, spiky script, were several sentences:

We must succeed at all costs.
We need to get to the truth, no matter what.
TRUTH ABOVE ALL!

The words didn't make sense. And yet, Brynn's whole body was trembling with fear—with *guilt*. Did she write this? What did she mean, *succeed at all costs*? What was happening to her? Why couldn't she remember this?

Click.

Brynn's spine straightened. What was that? She went to the window and peered out. The street was empty. There was no gray car.

She reached for her phone. The text was still on the screen: *you know you're one of us, if you dig deep.* Her brain started to hum. As though a curtain had just lifted in her mind, she saw herself saying those catchphrases. Yelling them, actually, at the top of her voice. Someone stood next to her, holding her hand tightly, urging her on. Brynn was pretty sure she knew who it was . . . but she couldn't make out a face.

And then she saw herself laughing. Saying, *Do you really think so?* Another voice saying, *C'mon. Just as an exercise. We'll never really do it.* And then she saw herself sketching something . . . but what? When she tried to hold on to the memory, it slipped through her hands, as cagey as a snake, maybe not real.

Another peal of laughter rang out from downstairs. Her mother's voice was melodic, and the famous interviewer's deep voice complimentary. Brynn covered her ears, too frazzled to listen. She wanted to close her eyes, too, but whenever she did, she kept seeing herself in that dark room from the past. She was saying words she didn't remember, making gestures she didn't recall, getting worked up over... *something*.

But the memory taunted her. It lifted the curtain to give her a glimpse ... but it didn't show her the whole picture. It didn't show her what that *something* she was getting worked up over was.

SEVEN

EIGHT DAYS TO LAUNCH

"So Jackson decides to record an epic video of him skating down the stone steps at Quiet Waters Park," Dex said as he grabbed another piece of fried zucchini from the big basket on the picnic table. "Of course he wipes out. It's a wonder he didn't crack his head open. The guy has never been on a skateboard in his life."

"Huh." Brynn's eyes nervously scanned the big restaurant space. It was Thursday, and they were at Growler's, a local place where you were just as likely to boat up to the establishment as park your car in the lot—even on a frigid late-fall day like this one. Waitresses swirled past with baskets of crab, lobster, fried shrimp, and garlic bread. The air smelled like Old Bay spice. But what was that shadow peering out from the back hall? Was that a person watching her? Brynn squinted hard. A waitress appeared through a swinging door carrying a tray. No one else.

"Brynn?"

Dex had his chin in his palm, and his brow was furrowed. "You're a million miles away. Hellooo? It's your boyfriend, Dex? Remember me?" He waved a hand in front of her face. His voice was light, but something in his face was not.

"I'm sorry." Brynn tried to smile and give him her full attention. "Go on. Tell me the rest."

Dex shrugged. "Well, do you want to see it?"

"See what?"

Dex's shoulders lowered. "Jackson's video. You *weren't* paying attention."

"I was," Brynn protested, though it was obvious she was lying. The contents of that USB drive thrummed in her mind like a heartbeat. She'd been too afraid to look at any of it again, but the files' impassioned sentences plagued her. Every time her phone beeped, she was sure it was *them*, contacting her again. Did they go by ACL, like the acronym on the drive's secret folder? What did that stand for? What did they want?

Should she confess? But what was she confessing *to*? She couldn't, not yet. Until she actually knew what the hell was happening, the fewer people who knew, the better.

The waitress set down their entrees. "Enjoy!"

Dex picked up his burger immediately. He didn't speak

to Brynn as he dug in; maybe he was ravenous, or maybe he was pouting because she'd been in her own world the whole date. Brynn was about to force herself to eat a bite of her meal when a dark flash in the door caught her eye. Lexi Gates had just come in with a few friends from studio art. They swept right past Brynn's table and settled into a long booth on the other side of the room. Most of the kids were chattering happily and looking at their menus, but as Lexi arranged her napkin on her lap, her gaze was steadily and unapologetically on Brynn. Her eyes were cold. Brynn looked away.

Dex followed her gaze. "Oh." His face soured at Lexi. "Did she just *glare* at you?"

Brynn flinched. "It doesn't matter."

"That's it." Dex shoved back his chair and stood. "I'm going to talk to her."

Brynn caught his arm. "Dex, no."

"I want to know what her deal is." Dex's jaw was tight. "She's being shady, and I'm sick of it."

"Dex," Brynn protested, but he was already across the room.

She watched as Dex leaned down and spoke to Lexi. Her old friend's face was a closed shell. Her eyebrows knit together, and she said something back to him, making a flippant gesture. A moment later, Dex was walking back to their table, his expression stony.

"What happened?" Brynn asked, her stomach churning.

Dex threw himself back into the booth and picked up his burger. "She said she had no idea what I was talking about. But hopefully she'll lose some of the bitchy attitude."

"You don't have to fight my battles."

Dex chewed vigorously. "I didn't like that comment she made about you in class."

"She was probably just trying to be funny. Maybe it was from something that happened this summer. Some inside joke I can't remember."

"Well, I told her it wasn't funny at all. It was mean."

"You didn't have to be mean back to her. Saying thermodynamics was a snoozefest?"

Dex frowned. "I thought you would have appreciated that."

"I appreciated that you stood up for me, but..." Brynn rubbed the spot between her eyes. She didn't mean to pick an argument with Dex. She peered across the room. Her old friend was whispering with the others, a mischievous expression on her face. Was she talking about her? Why did Lexi dislike her so much?

Brynn wished she remembered more about what had happened with Lexi, but it was a huge, dark hole. There was maybe a time when they met at the swimming pool ... and maybe they went for a run or two in the park ... but the meet-ups felt stilted, almost like something Brynn had to muddle through. And things were already frosty between them—it was clear Lexi didn't like Jacob. They never *did* meet. When Jacob broke up with her, Brynn felt like she couldn't cry on Lexi's shoulder. Lexi was probably happy Jacob was gone.

And then came this fight between them. Brynn recalled Lexi saying something scary, angry, mean. Brynn had stood on her porch, blocking Lexi's entry into the house. Lexi had glared at her, *hissing,* and then stormed away. What had they even been fighting about? Jacob, probably, though Brynn couldn't say for sure. It was funny how quickly an argument faded. The memory always just boiled down to emotions, how angry or betrayed you felt—not the actual words or who said what.

Brynn and Lexi never got together after that. By the time school began, they were strangers.

Despite all that, Brynn missed Lexi—badly. Sure, she had the other girls, friendships she'd rekindled since breaking up with Jacob, and then there were the new girls she'd met from Dex's cross-country team . . . but it wasn't the same. Lexi was special, and it was so heartbreaking that such an intense friendship could dissolve overnight. Who did Lexi turn to now to discuss the latest episode of *The Bachelor*? Was there a new friend who listened to her ideas for art projects or what her therapist said to her this week, or who knew that she was still haunted by the robbery? One time, two years ago, Lexi had fallen into such a funk that her parents had actually sent her to a "rest cure" for the weekend. Brynn had visited her, even sitting through an art therapy session in which Lexi drew her feelings in greasy crayon-pastels. When she'd left, Lexi had hugged her tightly, and Brynn could practically see Lexi's gratitude swirling around her, as if it were steam rising off a warm swimming pool.

"Look." Dex pointed at the TV screen over the small bar, interrupting Brynn's thoughts. A famous news program was on, and there was Rainer Wilson, his face weirdly orange from the HD makeup, his teeth gleaming white, his hair perfectly coiffed. As the camera pulled back, Brynn saw her own dining room—and then there was a shot of her mother and Dr. Lowell. She breathed in sharply. Here was the interview they'd done the day before yesterday. She had no idea it was going to make it onto TV this quickly.

"Whoa." Dex's gaze was glued to the TV. "Rainer Wilson was in your *house*? Why didn't you call me?"

Brynn rolled her jaw. "It was Tuesday night. Kind of unexpected."

"Did you meet him?"

"I wasn't in the mood."

Dex gawked at her like she was nuts. "You turned down meeting Rainer Wilson? That guy's a legend!"

"I was really tired. And he seemed sort of full of himself. Just took over our house with only a moment's notice. Who does that?"

"I'd let Rainer Wilson take over my house any day if it would mean I could get on his show." Dex got that pouty look again. "You really should have called me, Brynn. I would have loved a selfie!"

Brynn shrugged. Suddenly, she felt eyes on her from across the room. Lexi was watching her again. A jolt wriggled down Brynn's back. There was something so meaningful in Lexi's gaze, like she could read Brynn's addled mind. Brynn looked away, feigning interest in the TV. Someone had changed the channel, and now Senator Merriweather's face popped onto the screen. *Merriweather Wants to Bulk Up Interrogation Methods,* read the headline. At least four people sitting at the bar had stopped to pay attention. *We're too easy on terrorists,* read the senator's closed-captioned response. *These are people trying to destroy our way of life. We not only need to find out exactly what they know and what they plan to do, but it also might be worth trying to change the way they think. Explain to them that their ideology is a dead end. That there's no heaven after the explosion.*

"Jeez," Brynn murmured. She really didn't like thinking about suicide bombing.

"Brynn." Dex looked peeved. "You didn't hear anything I said *again*, did you?"

Brynn blinked at him, guilty. "I'm sorry. Lexi's throwing me off my game. And that guy isn't helping." She gestured at the senator on the screen, who was now in an argument with another talking head.

"Come on, then." Dex sounded defeated. "Maybe I should take you home early."

"You don't have to do that!" Brynn cried. It was only a little after seven P.M.; her parents weren't expecting her home until nine thirty.

"No. I need some time to myself. Maybe go for a late run." Without another word, Dex walked to the waitress stand to pay the check. Brynn grabbed her purse off the back of the chair, chastising herself for being so transparently absent. It wasn't Dex's fault her life had gotten very strange.

She rummaged inside her purse for a few bills to leave for a tip, then noticed a small slip of paper sticking out of the loose back pocket. Normally, she kept nothing in that pocket—it was so baggy, things always fell out. Her gaze fell on the unfamiliar handwriting on the front. *Brynn*.

She gulped, then looked around the room. Every table was full. The bartender noisily shook a martini. A toddler threw a toy airplane to the floor, and his mother picked it up. Lexi was listening to the girl next to her, but there was something distracted about her posture, like her attention was somewhere else.

Dex placed his hand on Brynn's arm, and she jumped. "What's that?"

He gestured at the note.

Brynn shoved it in her pocket. "Just some random receipt I found in my purse." She glanced over her shoulder once more. No one watched her, not even Lexi.

They rode home in near silence; Brynn could hear every clunk of the engine and rattle of the heater. At her curb, Dex gave her a tepid peck on the cheek and told her to feel better. Then he pulled back, looking guilty. "I need to tell you something."

Brynn felt a flutter of worry. "What?"

"Lexi said something else when I was at her table. At first I thought it wasn't worth repeating, but maybe you should know."

"Okay. . . ."

Dex stared at the steering wheel. "She said that I should watch out for you, because you have an unpredictable streak. That you can be really irrational. And angry."

It was so unexpected, Brynn burst out laughing. *"What?"*

He took her hands. "It's not like I believe it."

"But why would she *say* that?" Brynn asked breathlessly. She'd never, *ever* been like that around Lexi.

Had she? Her mind clicked back to the summer. That explosive fight on her porch. What had been said? Had she done something? All she remembered was feeling hurt, not what had actually happened.

"Don't worry about it, okay?" Dex gave her a tender smile. "And don't worry about *me*, either. Okay? I love you, no matter what. Even when you don't pay attention to me through dinner."

Brynn lowered her eyes. Normally, the sentiment would make her chuckle, but she felt too uneasy. "Okay," she mumbled. "Thanks."

"Listen, I have to get home. I'll see you tomorrow. Get

some rest." He cuffed her gently on the shoulder. "I'll retell you all the stuff that went in one ear and out the other before homeroom, okay?"

Brynn forced a laugh, gave him a kiss, and walked slowly to her house. Inside, the foyer was quiet, and there were no sounds from the dining room. No fancy interviews today, apparently.

She shut the door, pulled out her phone, and scrolled through for Lexi's number. Why would Lexi *say* that? What did she have against Brynn, and why was she trying to sabotage things with her and Dex? Mustering up her courage, she pressed Call. The phone rang once, then twice. On the third ring, someone picked up. At first, there was just breathing, but Brynn could tell Lexi was there.

Brynn swallowed hard. "H-Hey."

"Hello." Lexi's voice was guarded.

Brynn's nerves snapped. *Just ask.* But how would Lexi answer? What if Brynn *had* done something irrational or crazy? Still, she had to know. She took a deep breath. "Listen, Lexi, about tonight—"

"I hope you're happy, Brynn," Lexi interrupted, her voice sharp, definite. "I really hope you're happy."

"Huh?" Brynn cried. But Lexi had already hung up.

She stared at the phone for a moment, dumbfounded. What did *that* mean? Why had her old friend sounded so . . . *bitter*? She rooted in her memory, desperate for anything . . . but nothing came.

She dropped her phone into her pocket, and her fingers grazed against paper. The note from the restaurant. She'd forgotten.

Brynn could hear her heart thudding in her ears as she pulled the folded note out of her pocket. The paper crinkled as she unfolded it. Written inside were only a few words.

> Mrs. Dalloway. *Eastport Public Library.*
> *You'll find answers to who we are—who*
> YOU *are—there.*

Brynn blinked. *Who we are.* The people behind her mystery texts? And that title had significance—but it took her a few moments to remember why. It was a relief to remember; her memory couldn't be *that* bad. But then she straightened with a jolt.

Mrs. Dalloway was Jacob's favorite book.

EIGHT

At eleven P.M., Brynn hefted up her bedroom window and stared at the dark shingle roof. It was sloped in such a way that if she shimmied down to the gutter, she wouldn't have to drop very far to the ground. This was the only way to get out of the house without alerting her parents or disabling the noisy security system. The last time she'd snuck out was in her Jacob days. That didn't conjure up very pleasant memories, but Jacob was already on her mind tonight.

She held her breath and squeezed out the window. The shingles were rougher than she remembered, scraping against her knees. The air was downright chilly, too; she was glad she'd brought her down coat. As quietly as she could, she inched along the roof, praying a neighbor wouldn't notice. Last year, her father had caught her sneaking out. Brynn had made an excuse that she'd forgotten her homework at Lexi's house and didn't want to wake them. Luckily, he hadn't found out she was actually off to see Jacob in town. Her dad didn't even *know* she had a boyfriend; Jacob wasn't really one to schmooze with parents. And he'd been furious when she hadn't shown up that night. He'd refused to call her for three whole days.

Did the book clue mean Jacob was behind the weird texts? Why? She looked at them again. The number was a scrambled mess of ones and zeroes, but when she'd written back before, someone had responded. She decided to give it another try. *Is this Jacob?* she typed.

An answer came almost immediately. *I don't know who you're talking about. Stop asking questions.* Brynn wasn't sure if she believed that response—it was too quick, too defensive. It actually sounded like something Jacob might say.

The streets were eerily quiet, all of the houses dark. A few blocks to the north, laughs rang out from one of the bars, but the sounds quickly died away. The block the library was on was shrouded in trees. Not a single car was in the parking lot. Something fluttered out of the corner of Brynn's eye, and she swiftly turned to see what it was. A tiny mouse skittered from behind a dumpster. Brynn silently watched as its tail disappeared into the grass.

She crept up to the library window and looked inside

through the glass door. The lights were off. There were neat lines in the carpet where someone had run a vacuum, and all of the stuffed animal puppets, which kids usually made a mess of during regular hours, were tucked inside their box on the librarian's desk. Brynn had spent countless hours at this branch after school and in the summer, and last year she'd even volunteered here, leading story hours and collecting fees for overdue books. That was how she knew about the jammed window at the very back near the reference section; Mrs. Dawes, the head librarian, kept saying she was going to call a handyman to get the thing fixed, but Brynn bet she still hadn't gotten around to it. Heart thudding, she crept through the grass until she reached the window in question. *Bingo.* It still stood about a foot open, letting in the drafty air. It was just wide enough for her to squeeze through.

She stared at her pale hands curled around the window sash. Her knuckles looked knobby and garish. Was she really going to do this? Was following this clue important enough to break into a building for? What on earth would her parents say if they caught her? Should she wait until morning?

The vision of being interrogated flashed before her eyes again. *Tell us what you know.* Whatever that was, it had to be connected to the strange texts—Brynn could *feel* it. If she didn't get to the bottom of this tonight, she wouldn't be able to sleep. And what if tomorrow was too late?

Using her arms, she pressed herself against the jamb,

wriggled her head and shoulders through the gap in the window, and awkwardly shimmied the rest of the way, tumbling to the ground with a *thud*. She lay still for a moment, waiting for alarms to sound, but nothing happened.

It was so dark inside the library that Brynn could barely see the shelves, but she knew the layout well enough to recall that adult fiction was on the other side of the large square room. She crawled on her hands and knees across the carpet. The air smelled pleasantly like dust and books. A poster for the newest *Harry Potter* spinoff was taped to Mrs. Dawes's desk. She passed the water fountain, the computer terminals, the printers, and then the door to the children's books. Over her head, she noticed a steady red beam of light on what looked to be a security camera. She gulped. Was it recording her right now?

She ducked her head down. She wasn't sure if the camera could record images at night, but she didn't want to take any chances. The fiction section was ahead, and she crawled faster. Once behind the stacks, she slowly rose to her feet. Her vision adjusted to the darkness, and she could make out the titles on the spines. The shelf for Virginia Woolf, *Mrs. Dalloway*'s author, was a few rows down. The library had a healthy Woolf section. Brynn's eyes scanned the titles. *To the Lighthouse. The Waves. A Room of One's Own.* And then, there it was, the last book at the very bottom. Brynn grabbed the book from the shelf, only noticing when it was halfway out that a long, thin piece of paper, sort of like a bookmark, protruded from between the pages. It fluttered to the ground like a discarded tissue, but even in the darkness, Brynn could read what was written on it in thick black ink. BRYNN CALDWELL.

Bile rose in her throat.

She crouched and picked it up. There was nothing else written on it except for her name. She turned the book over and looked at the cover. It bore a picture of two women in bell-sleeved white dresses and large sunhats. Brynn recalled reading *Mrs. Dalloway* in English class; it was about a woman's day, with something about her husband and lover, and then a side plot about a mentally ill man, Septimus. She'd written a paper about Septimus, in fact, but with all the books she'd had to read for English, she couldn't remember what was significant about him. Literary fiction had always been Jacob's thing. He could quote lines from *Mrs. Dalloway* by heart, and he'd ribbed Brynn for not understanding the book's nuances.

"Hello?"

Brynn's head shot up just in time to see a beam of light sweeping the room.

"Annapolis Police," the same voice called. "Anyone here?"

Brynn's stomach did a flip. Her limbs turned to ice.

There was a footstep, then a jingling sound. "We got a call that someone was seen crawling through a window. If someone is here, come out with your hands up."

Stuffing the book into her messenger bag, Brynn shot

through the stacks. Her footsteps echoed through the space, and she bumped into a metal cart.

"Hey!" The cop's voice was gruffer. "Stop!"

Brynn had to get out of here *now*. She could hear his footsteps behind her; soon enough, he would round the corner and *see* her, and it would all be over. Her legs burned. Her heart pounded. She sprinted for the open window. When she reached it, she wriggled through quickly, barely registering how the sash bumped against her spine and how her sleeve tore on the jagged crank. She rolled onto the dirt outside just in time to see the cop barrel around the tall shelf and straight for the window. She scrambled away and pressed herself against the building underneath the sash. In seconds, he would run over here, look out, and spy her. She was trapped.

"Come on," a low voice whispered.

Brynn felt a hand pull her to stand. Suddenly, thick smoke surrounded her face, and her lungs filled. She began to cough. The man pulling her launched through the grass, and Brynn scrambled to keep up. They ran for many feet in the stinky smoke, but then the grass grew wetter and thicker, and the smoke dissipated into thin wisps. Brynn could see thick, tall trees all around her, and she realized they'd run all the way to the woods behind the library.

Brynn turned back to the building. A large cloud of smoke now filled the parking lot, nearly covering the white-and-black squad car at the entrance. "Hey!" she heard the cop yell, though she couldn't see him. "Hello?" He sounded angry. "Come out!"

Brynn stared down at her hand. Whoever had pulled her out of this wasn't holding it anymore. Breathing hard, she spun around, apprehensive at who she might see. When a familiar face came into view, she stifled a surprised yelp.

Dex.

NINE

D
ex's brow was creased. His normally clear blue eyes were stormy. He scanned Brynn cautiously, as though afraid to look at her fully.

"W-What are you doing here?" Brynn stammered.

"I could ask you the same thing," Dex said. "Why are you breaking into the library at eleven o'clock at night?"

Brynn ran her hand over her forehead. The noxious smoke still hung in the air, making her eyes water. "Did you follow me? A-And how did you make it get so smoky?"

"You've been acting strangely for days now. I decided to drive by your house tonight, maybe see if you wanted to talk. Then I saw you drop off your roof. At first I thought you were sneaking out to meet another guy." His voice cracked.

Brynn licked her lips. All at once, she felt ashamed.

Dex gestured to the clearing smoke. "It's just a smoke bomb. I had one in my car—it was supposed to be for Jackson's skateboard video—and when I saw the cop pull up, I thought it might come in handy." He made a small noise of disbelief. "What was in there that was so important? The police were after you. You could have gotten caught. Thrown in jail. For someone who's desperate to get a college scholarship... You don't want a *record*, do you?"

The wind gusted, chilling Brynn to her core. On one hand, she appreciated that her boyfriend was concerned about her. On the other, she hated how this all must look from Dex's vantage point. She fully understood she was acting strange... and yet, right now, she didn't know how else *to* act. It was arduous to handle this alone. Practically impossible.

She sniffed loudly, suddenly feeling tears coming on. "I can't tell you," she blurted out. "It's better that you don't know."

At first, she could sense Dex stiffening, maybe ramping up to get mad. But then he sighed. "Brynn. Come on. You're obviously struggling with something. Just say what's on your mind."

His eyes gleamed in the moonlight. His face looked soft, kind, caring, like all he wanted was to throw a big blanket around her and protect her forever. Brynn sobbed. Keeping this inside felt *painful,* like a breath held way too long. She needed to let it out.

She took a deep gulp of air, and then it all came out of her—the panic attacks, the notes she'd received, the car she'd seen at the cemetery, the extremely vivid dream about being kidnapped, and the mysterious files on the USB drive.

"It's like whoever is texting me is trying to clue me in to my own life, but it's details I have no recollection of," she finished. "And tonight, they sent me here, to get a book." She patted her messenger bag. "They said it would explain who they were, and who I was. But I don't know why."

Dex blinked hard. He looked dumbstruck. "You have no idea who is sending you these messages?"

Brynn stared up at the moon for a few beats. She hated what she had to say next, especially because she wasn't even sure she believed it. "Maybe it's Jacob."

He made a face. "Your ex?"

"I don't know. But this was his favorite book." She undid the flap of her bag and showed him *Mrs. Dalloway.*

Dex looked uneasy. "What would *he* want?"

"It seems like he's reminding me of something we were involved in together. And it seems like some sort of event is going to happen. The texts keep saying *it's almost time* and *ten more days*." Brynn explained the impassioned phrases from the USB drive's file, too.

"*Truth above all?*" Dex said. He sounded incredulous. "That sounds a little revolutionary."

Brynn scoffed. "You think we're going to stage a coup?"

"Or maybe you're part of a terror cell."

She started to laugh . . . but Dex didn't look like he was kidding. "Uh, I don't think so," she said. Dex still didn't crack a smile. "Dex," Brynn said, suddenly feeling uneasy. "Come on. You really think *I'd* be in a terror cell?"

He wouldn't look at her. "You were in a controlling relationship, Brynn. Who's to say Jacob didn't force you into doing something really extreme?"

Brynn stared at him, aghast. "I was still *myself*. I mean, yeah, I did idiotic things like sneak out, and I slacked off in school, but I didn't go completely bonkers and join something like ISIS." She laughed self-consciously. "And look, even though Jacob isn't high on my list of favorite people right now, I can't see him joining ISIS, either."

"Not ISIS, necessarily, but maybe something more homegrown?" Dex stared down at his hands. "Earnest and well-meaning, even? Citizens hoping to create change?"

"By violence?" Brynn touched her chest. "I can't believe it. You really think *I'm* violent. Is this because of what Lexi told you about me?"

Dex squeezed his eyes shut. "It's just . . . you said you can't remember a lot from this summer. What if you got sucked into something really bad?"

Brynn stared at him. It felt like her heart was breaking in two. He really thought she was capable of something awful.

She turned away, feeling bitter, hurt, and confused. The smoke had cleared completely, and the cop was climbing into his car and saying something into his walkie-talkie. Brynn watched as he started the engine and drove away. "If I did join a terror cell, it wasn't with Jacob," she muttered. "We broke up in June. He wasn't around."

"Are you *sure*, Brynn?"

Brynn clenched her jaw. *Was* she sure? Yes. Or, well, she was *almost* sure. What was with the strange coincidence about the book? And Dex was right—of everyone in Brynn's life, Jacob was the only person who had ever had control over her. And the weird thing was, it *did* feel like there was something lurking in her subconscious that was maybe . . . illicit. Even . . . *dangerous*?

No. *No.* It wasn't possible. She wasn't a violent person. Not in the throes of depression, not in her Lost Puppy Dog Jacob phase, *never.* Being a terrorist meant *hurting* people. It meant having no respect for human life. She squared her shoulders. "Yes. I'm sure."

Dex's gaze fell to her bag. "So why did someone leave you that book?"

"I don't know." Brynn opened the flap and pulled out the copy of *Mrs. Dalloway*. Its library binding crinkled, and a musty scent wafted out. Her fingers touched the thin, yellowed pages. They were almost translucent. When she flipped to the back, another piece of paper fluttered to the ground. Something had been folded up and shoved into the book. Brynn picked it up and unfolded it, but her vision blurred, and she didn't understand at first what she was looking at.

"Brynn." Dex's voice was choked. "This is your writing."

Brynn struggled to make sense of what was on the page. At the top were scrawls of numbers and random words she didn't remember writing in her small, spiky script. On the sides were equations and calculations. But it was the drawing itself that stopped her cold. It was the same octagonal shape she'd been drawing for days, though the shape on this sheet of paper looked like some sort of circuit board, red and green and black lines connecting squares to other squares. Her gaze stopped on the words *9 Volt* and a crude drawing of a battery. There was a small rectangle that read *Clock*. She squinted at the words *SPDT RELAY* in the middle, and then *Boom* at the top left.

The puzzle pieces snapped into shape in Brynn's mind. She staggered back, a hand to her mouth. Her memory flipped back to a vignette of her laughing with someone, spreading some sort of machinery out on a table. And someone saying, *Just draw it as an exercise. Just draw it so I can see what it looks like.* And, despite her better instincts, leaning over to sketch this familiar shape on a piece of paper—exactly like the one she was holding now.

Her eyes met Dex's. His cheeks looked hollow. His pupils were huge. "Is that what I think it is?" he said hoarsely.

Brynn nodded, her heart rocketing. "I-It's a bomb."

TEN

"Wait." Dex stepped back from her, nearly tripping over a tree root. He held his hands at his chest as though to shield himself. "Brynn. What the hell?"

Brynn stared at the paper in her hands. She badly wanted to tell Dex that they'd made a mistake, that this was a schematic for something else. But that would have been a lie. She would have known what the drawing was even if she hadn't done the report on bombs for Chang's class. Thermodynamics, the chemistry and physics of explosion and change—a.k.a. the science of weapons of mass destruction—were the subjects that most excited her. She read books about the Manhattan Project for fun. But she'd never actually *designed* one.

Or had she?

A cold, sick feeling spread through her gut. She might not remember why she'd drawn this, but she certainly could have done it. It made no sense. *How could she have done this?* What had happened to her? Who *was* she?

"Brynn." Dex stared at her as though he'd never seen her before in his life. He looked afraid. "What did you do?"

"I—I didn't draw this." But as soon as the words came out of her mouth, she didn't feel so sure. "I mean . . . I might have, but maybe it was for school or something. Like an experiment." Her mouth felt dry, her throat tight. When she looked up at him, her eyes filled with desperate tears. "I'm not a terrorist, Dex. I promise."

Dex didn't say anything. He was staring at the left corner of the page that read *Boom*.

Brynn prodded at the memory she'd just half seen, begging for it to uncurl. At present, it was only that small, flickering light in her mind; she saw a laugh, a pen to paper, and heard herself saying, *It's not like we'll do it for real.* What did it mean? Who was she talking to? Maybe she'd never intended to do anything evil? Even so, she'd drawn this. She'd thought about how to set it off; she'd calculated its force and depth of damage. She stared down at her hands as though they belonged to a stranger.

Maybe Dex sensed these questions, because suddenly he stepped so far away that his back butted against a tree. He reached for his phone. "I need to call the cops."

"No!" She lunged for him. "Please! You can't!"

His eyes flashed. "Why not?"

"Because it's just a drawing. It doesn't *mean* anything. Just wait for me to figure this out, okay? There has to be more to the story that I can't remember."

He held the phone to his chest. "When I interned for the NSA, they taught me that behavior like yours, coupled with the notes you just showed me and those texts, would be enough to file a report on you for suspicious activity."

Brynn was horrified. "But you know me! I'm not some terrorist!"

Dex peered at her hard, looking like he didn't quite believe her. "Okay, what's Jacob's number? Obviously he's the one who talked you into this. I should turn him in, too."

"Dex, wait. We don't know if Jacob's behind this."

"So now you're protecting him?"

Brynn pressed her hands to her eyes. When had everything gotten so out of control? "I don't know what I'm doing. I can't *remember*. You have to believe me."

He pressed his lips together. "I don't know, Brynn. I really don't know. This is serious."

Brynn wiped the tears from her face. "I thought talking to you was safe, that you would help me."

"I didn't realize we were dealing with bombs. I *am* helping you."

Brynn looked away, feeling sick. Maybe she couldn't blame Dex for that reaction.

"Does this bomb exist?" Dex asked quietly, after a moment.

Brynn tried to remember, but it was useless. "I wish I knew."

The moonlight seemed to darken, casting long shadows over Dex's face. He met her gaze for a moment, then wrenched his eyes away. "Look, I won't call the police. But that's only because I care about you. Still, I need you to do the right thing. If there's a bomb out there, if there's going to be an attack...well, I need you to turn yourself in." Brynn opened her mouth to protest, and he cut her off. "I'll give you twenty-four hours to figure out what's going on. If you haven't called the authorities by then, I'm going to call them myself."

"And say what?" she argued. *"Hey, I found this bomb schematic I'm pretty sure my girlfriend drew."*

"I don't know. Maybe."

Panic rose in Brynn's chest. "Will you help me figure out what's going on?"

His eyes widened. *"Me?"*

"Of course you. I can't do it alone. And I certainly don't want to tell anyone else."

"No way." He started across the lawn, back toward the library. "You're on your own."

Brynn's mouth fell open. An hour ago, Dex would have done anything for her. Now he was looking at her like a stranger. "Dex, wait!" she cried.

But he was already halfway across the parking lot.

"Twenty-four hours, Brynn," he called over his shoulder. "That's it."

Hot, confused tears filled Brynn's eyes. She watched Dex's dark shape disappear past the smoke and around the library, praying he'd turn back to her, come to his senses. He *had* to believe she wasn't evil. He *had* to believe this was all some sort of awful misunderstanding.

A car engine roared to life. Headlights shone across the pavement, and she caught sight of Dex in the driver's seat of his Jeep, his jaw set, his eyes fixed on the road. Brynn bent her head down, feeling like she was going to shatter. Her whole world was ripped open, burned, *destroyed*. Nothing felt real. She could hear herself sobbing, but the sounds were foreign, strange—not hers at all.

But maybe that made sense. Because she didn't *know* herself anymore. Because, suddenly, she was a terrifying, unpredictable stranger.

ELEVEN

SEVEN DAYS TO LAUNCH

As Thursday night eased into Friday morning, Brynn lost track of time. She lay curled in a ball on her bed, the covers over her, but sleep didn't come. It felt like she was falling deeper, deeper, deeper into a bottomless well. All around her, voices were shouting. *You're worthless. You're nothing. Dex hates you now, just like Jacob hated you then. You should have stuck with Jacob, should have been a better girlfriend. He could have kept you in line. But you weren't good enough for him. You aren't good enough for anyone.*

"Stop!" she screamed, pressing the heels of her hands to her temples.

After what seemed like hours, she felt a little better. She sat up in bed and looked around. The room was dark but cozy. Safe. The voices were gone, thankfully, and the only sound was the whir of her desk fan. *Whoa,* she thought. Had her head really gone to such a crazy, dark place? It had been a long time since she'd actually *longed* for Jacob. That was insane, obviously—Jacob hadn't been good to her. She *knew* that. It wasn't because she wasn't good enough for him.

She rolled her head around on her neck, waking up her muscles. The confusion of everything that was happening made her head hurt. Her crazed thoughts, those panicked memories, her inability to sleep—it all felt like her depression returning. Then something hit her: What if it was just her body weaning off antidepressants? The doctor had warned her that side effects could happen if she weaned off too quickly; in some kids, depressive thoughts could return. She pulled her knees to her chest, feeling a bolt of fear. Should she go back on the pills just in case?

Then she remembered everything she'd learned about herself in the last day—which, coupled with whatever was going on inside her body, was enough to put her in a tailspin. She leapt up from the bed and started to search her room. In mere minutes, every single book on her shelf lay open on the floor. The contents of her drawers were in a pile on her bed. She'd even removed the plate covering the heating vent to root around in the dust. But none of it had yielded clues to what was going on. She still had no way of proving she wasn't a terrorist.

A terrorist. Someone who's evil. Someone who's awful. Someone who kills. Could it possibly be true?

Brynn clicked on Facebook, searching her page for clues from the spring and summer. Was that when she'd made that drawing of the bomb? But her posts back then had been sparse; Jacob didn't like when she posted on social media. He said it was narcissistic.

Jacob. Brynn shut her eyes and tried to picture his face, but only saw his eye rolls, his crooked, taunting smile, a slash of dark hair. Maybe Dex was right—he *had* to be involved. He was the only person who could force her into something like this. But why? And why had she gone along with it? *And why couldn't she remember?*

After she started dating Dex, she told him that she'd cut Jacob off completely, deleting him from her social media accounts, erasing his phone number from her contacts list, et cetera. But it wasn't quite the truth. Her gaze shifted to the shoebox on her carpet. It was filled with love letters from Jacob. They were like poetry, sweet little blooms of affection that wound around her heart and pulled tight. Brynn had wanted to get rid of them, but she couldn't. This morning, she'd forced herself to reread every single one, but even they hadn't sparked new memories.

Except for one thing. A couple of the love letters had been sent via email, and though Brynn had made it a point to forget Jacob's address, it had been right there on top of the printouts she had saved. Jacob might not use the account anymore—it was just a silly Gmail address with a made-up handle, not even his name—but it wouldn't hurt just to make sure. Out of options, she composed a new message.

> It's Brynn. Look, if it really is you texting me, just tell me. You might not realize, but I actually don't remember what happened. I won't get you in trouble. Just tell me yes or no.

Did that give away too much? Brynn wasn't sure, but she didn't know how to edit it down. She pressed Send before she lost her nerve.

She clicked back to her page on Facebook. As she scrolled into the fall, posts popped up more frequently. One was a photo of her and Dex at their favorite sushi restaurant. *Dex*, she thought with an ache, staring at his smiling face pressed up to hers in the picture. Would things ever be the same between them again?

Biting hard on her lip, she tried Dex's phone. Voice mail. She didn't leave a message. *Please call me,* she texted. *Let's work together for the next twenty-four hours. If we can't find anything, then I'll call the cops. Turn myself in. I promise. I don't want anyone getting hurt, either.*

A knock sounded at the door. Brynn shoved her phone under her pillow, but before she could tell her parents to go away, they pushed the door open and stepped inside.

"Oh," Mr. Caldwell said quickly, his eyes widening at

the mess. The complete contents of Brynn's trash can, empty chip bags included, lay on the carpet as though her room were now a garbage dump.

"What happened in here?" Dr. Caldwell asked.

"I—I was looking for something," Brynn said, fully aware of how lame that sounded. "I'll clean it up."

"You look like you haven't slept." Dr. Caldwell stepped into Brynn's room, carefully avoiding a lamp that had been knocked over. Normally, her parents didn't mind a little mess, but they both looked really worried.

"We can help, if you want," her dad said, picking up a sheet of paper from the bed. Brynn's heart stopped when she realized what it was. *The drawing of the bomb.*

"No!" she said quickly, snatching it from his fingers and stuffing it into her desk drawer. She slammed the drawer shut and felt a prickle of anger. "Can you guys please give me a little space?"

Her parents exchanged a loaded glance. Brynn's heart sank. *Oh no.* She'd gone too far.

Her mother cleared her throat. "Are you okay, honey?"

Brynn turned away. "Yep. Totally fine."

They fell silent. Both looked tired and uneasy, but Brynn thought she detected something else in their faces, too. A strange sort of awareness. An awkwardness she'd never noticed before.

Could they *know*? Brynn's mind swirled. Could they have guessed that Brynn had been up to something last spring? Maybe they'd figured out something she hadn't yet. Her skin began to prickle. Maybe it made sense. They had friends who worked for the CIA, the NSA, the FBI. Friends who probably knew the warning signs of an attack.

Was she some kind of terrorist?

"Would you stop *staring* at me?" she snapped, flopping down on her bed. "It's freaking me out."

"Sorry." Mr. Caldwell pushed aside some pencils Brynn had dumped onto the bed and sat down next to her. Dr. Caldwell plopped down on the other side, placing a hand on Brynn's knee. Normally, their close proximity calmed her, made her feel loved. But today it felt like an unwanted ambush.

"You know, honey, when I was in graduate school, there was a spot in the Baltimore symphony I wanted very, very badly," Mr. Caldwell said. "I loved the conductor. I loved the pieces they were going to play. So I rehearsed my heart out. I was sure I was going to get it. But then I got a call saying someone else had gotten the job. I was crushed. I couldn't believe they hadn't picked me. But you know what? It just made me work harder. And that's what you'll do, too."

Brynn drew in a breath. *Oh.* They thought this was about the Dove award. That was all. She felt relieved . . . but also kind of disappointed. Were her parents really so blind? But still, this she could deal with.

"Dad, stop," she moaned. "You've told me that story a thousand times."

"He's just trying to make you feel better," Dr. Caldwell said. "Everyone makes mistakes. Even your dad. Even me."

Brynn snorted. "Uh, *no*. You're perfect. Never made a mistake in your life. So don't try that one on me."

Her dad made a strange face. He met her mom's gaze, and she looked away. Brynn suddenly felt a curious flicker of something unsaid.

"What?" she asked.

"Nothing," her mom said quickly.

"Celeste, maybe you should tell her," Brynn's father said. "This is a teachable moment."

"Tell me what?" Brynn asked, her heart speeding up a little. "What's going on?"

Dr. Caldwell tugged at her collar, something she always did when she was anxious. "Fine," she said, sounding peeved. "Okay. I got into Harvard when I was seventeen, a whole year early—"

"Wait, you went to Harvard?" Brynn interrupted. Her mom had always told her she'd gone to MIT.

"I'm getting to that," Dr. Caldwell said quietly. "I only went for a year. It had always been my dream to go, but the pressure was intense. Everyone was so, so smart... and I wasn't sure I could keep up. And so..." Her shoulders heaved. She looked positively tortured. "I stole another student's results and turned them in as my own."

"You did *what*?" Brynn felt sick.

Her mother lowered her eyes. Her face had turned red. She shot her husband a look.

"It's okay, Celeste," he urged.

"It was a terrible mistake, obviously," Brynn's mother muttered. "My lab partner, this girl named Carlie, caught me. She said she wouldn't tell . . . if I never did it again. I guess I trusted her . . . but at the same time, I felt like I needed a fresh start. A do-over. So I switched to MIT. I never put Harvard on my résumé. I'd rather just . . . forget about it."

"Mom!" Brynn cried, horrified.

"We all have ups and downs," Brynn's father jumped in. "No one is one hundred percent good and makes one hundred percent right decisions all the time."

Brynn licked her lips. All of a sudden, she was shaking. "But you told no one," she said to her mom.

Dr. Caldwell nodded. "Only your father."

"But no one at your job. You never put it on a résumé."

Her mother shifted uncomfortably. "Well, it's never come up."

"And you never told *me*, either."

Her mother looked up at her sheepishly. Brynn could feel the anger blazing beneath her skin. Dr. Caldwell moved to speak, but Brynn cut her off. "I go through this huge episode with you guys last summer. I bare my soul, I take meds, I go to a doctor, and all the while, I still think you're *perfect*, Mom. Like you'd never lie, you'd never get depressed, you'd never have a setback. Because you *let* me think that. And now I find out it's all a lie."

Her father's eyes widened. Her mother gasped. "Honey!" she said. "My life is *not* a lie!"

"How do I know?" Brynn cried. "Who knows what's true anymore?" She backed away from her parents until she was almost pressed up against the window. She couldn't contain her emotions; she felt a rush of desperate confusion. It felt like her whole world was crumbling. Her mind, her identity—and now she didn't know who her family was, either. "Would you have even told me if Dad hadn't forced it out of you? What *else* don't I know?"

Brynn's mother stepped toward her. "I'm sorry. This isn't that big of a deal. You're blowing it out of proportion."

"You should have told me. Considering I *idolized* you. Considering I wanted to follow in your footsteps."

Dr. Caldwell stared at her feet for a moment, nervously chewing on one of her fingernails. "I'll be much more open with you going forward. I promise. But listen, you won't mention this at the Cortexia launch, will you? That probably isn't the right time to discuss it."

Brynn's head shot up. "Are you for *real*?"

Dr. Caldwell held her hands in front of her body in surrender. "I just thought I should check—"

"Get out," Brynn snapped, turning away from them. She could feel the tears so close to the surface. "Go to work, as that's clearly where your priorities lie."

"Brynn!" Mr. Caldwell cried. "You're out of line!"

"It's all right," Dr. Caldwell murmured. "Just let her be."

Brynn's head was turned away, but she could hear them shifting and shuffling, then opening the door. She thought they were gone, but then there was a rap on the door frame. She glanced over her shoulder. Her father stood in the doorway, an envelope in his hand.

"This was on the doorstep," he said in a low tone, forcefully winging the envelope onto her bed. "And if I were you, I'd apologize to your mother."

Brynn didn't answer, instead hunching her shoulders and hugging herself even harder. He finally sighed and shut the door.

She turned and stared at the envelope on the bed. BRYNN CALDWELL, it read on the front in generic typed font. There was no postmark, no stamp. Whoever had sent this had dropped it off personally.

Brynn's chest felt like it was going to explode. Her phone beeped, telling her she had a text. She pulled it out from under her pillow. *Fine,* Dex had replied. *Twenty-four hours. Meet me at Bertell's Coffee Co. this afternoon after school.*

Brynn shivered with relief. *Thank God.* The plan for a rendezvous made her feel brave, so she picked up the letter. Her fingers shook as she slid her nail under the glue on the back of the envelope. Inside was something on heavy cardstock. She shook the envelope, and the card fell out, faceup.

You are formally invited to the launch and gala of
Cortexia at the BioXin Building Atrium.
Sponsored by BioXin Labs.
Black tie. Dinner at 7.

Brynn stared. There was no reason for her to receive an invite—she was Dr. Caldwell's daughter and therefore already going. Then she turned the invitation over. Taped to the back was a pink Post-it with ACL printed at the top and looping letters marching across the bottom.

T-minus one week. Be ready.

Brynn's heart stopped. She leapt up, a horrible idea suddenly seizing her. It took only a few clicks on her computer to find information about the BioXin building, and then a few more clicks to locate a PDF of its floor plan. She'd seen that floor plan before. Of course she had.

The puzzle pieces had slotted into place, making a noxious picture. The invitation fluttered to the floor.

"*No!*" she whispered.

The bomb was for the Cortexia launch.

TWELVE

Brynn had never been a fan of Bertell's Coffee Co., which was nestled on a side street that bordered the harbor; played obscure, trendy music; sold drinks that were underwhelming at ten dollars a pop; and was mostly the hangout of the beautiful, wealthy high school crowd whose parents owned houses on the water and huge yachts in the boatyards. She knew some of those kids, of course—and some of them were quite nice—but she was happy that she didn't see any of them today. What she did notice, as she stood just inside the door, was Senator Merriweather on TV again, this time talking about some new stealth bomber he was encouraging the Senate to approve. Man, it seemed like that guy was *everywhere*.

She looked around, her hands still trembling. When she noticed Dex sitting alone in one of the back booths, her stomach did a flip. Their eyes met. Dex nodded, then looked away. Rolling back her shoulders, she started toward him. As she sat down—across from Dex, and careful not to automatically reach out for his hand—she took a breath. "Thanks for coming."

Dex's eyes darted back and forth. "I still think we should call the police."

A squeal rose up from the vintage pinball machine at the back of the room, and they both glanced that way. Brynn cleared her throat. "I think someone is planning to blow up the Cortexia launch next week . . . and I might have been helping them."

Dex's head snapped up. *"What?"*

She handed over the invitation and the accompanying Post-it. Dex's eyes widened.

Brynn tapped the pink note. *"ACL* could stand for Anti-Cortexia League."

Dex had turned pale. "So that blueprint you talked about outside the library, the one you found on that flash drive. It's the BioXin building, isn't it?"

"Yes." Brynn's eyes dropped to the table. "That was one of the first things I looked at again after I got this invitation. All the exits are circled, maybe looking for a clean getaway—or a place to hide the . . . you know."

"The bomb." Dex looked horrified.

Shame wrapped around her like a scarf. *Yes, the bomb.* But whenever she tried to imagine herself plotting to hurt people, her mind just hit a roadblock. Such a scenario seemed so impossible.

"Maybe we were going to warn them," she said quietly, hopefully. "But anyway, I think it's why that guy in my memory was grilling me for answers. Maybe he was the leader of ACL and eager to find out what I knew about Cortexia. Maybe he figured I'd have insider knowledge since I'm Celeste Caldwell's daughter. And maybe he forced me to help them. Like threatened he'd kill my parents or something if I didn't."

"But if they forced you, then why did the text say you were one of them?" Dex asked.

"I don't know. Maybe they're just trying to manipulate me. Make me believe I sided with them, even though I was forced."

"Or maybe Jacob convinced you it was a good idea."

Brynn felt a flare of anger. "I might have been under Jacob's thumb, but I wouldn't have joined a protest group against my mother's work simply because my boyfriend told me to." There was a wobble in her voice. Brynn wanted to believe she still knew herself, still trusted herself, but the ground felt so shaky.

"Look, Cortexia is a good medication." She laid her

hands flat on the table to drive the point home. "My mom had only the best intentions when she created it. To think I could protest against her . . . try to *kill* her—"

"What if you found out something awful about the drug?" Dex asked.

"I wish I remembered," Brynn said. "But it's just *gone*. I was so mired in the depression. Do you think I was just so wiped out I forgot everything?"

"Maybe," Dex said.

She drummed her fingers on the table. "I thought those IP addresses on the USB drive could be a clue. Turns out they link to computers belonging to soldiers who were in the clinical trials who created personal blog sites and crowd-funding pages. I read through almost all of them, and all of the guys had a good experience on Cortexia. They got the shots, they talked with therapists, and slowly their take on the memories wasn't as traumatic. It was a long process— some of them had to go to tons of appointments to get through all the memories, and then the therapists had to carefully work on those memories to change the way the patients viewed them, but in the end, everyone was cured of PTSD."

"Okay, so what about that page of notes? All those for-mulas? Maybe that explains what's wrong with Cortexia?"

Brynn shook her head. "No, they're for the bomb design." She hated saying the word *bomb* out loud. "I don't want to think it exists . . . but if these people are saying, *It's almost time, get ready*, then maybe it does. But I don't know *why*. There's *nothing* wrong with Cortexia as far as I can see. It's like . . . the perfect medication."

Dex leaned back in the booth. "Do you think this protest group has tried to get to your mom? Do you remember any protestors in front of her lab, people sending her hate mail, anything like that?"

"No. *No.*" Brynn blinked hard. "Everyone *loves* my mom. She's never done anything to make anyone angry in her entire life." But then, with a jolt, she thought about what her mom had confessed just that morning. Stealing data from other students. Running away from Harvard. Still, that was a long time ago. A time her mom wanted to forget about.

"Say Jacob was involved." Dex interrupted her thoughts. "Do you remember him asking a lot of questions about Cortexia? Or expressing his disapproval of your mom?"

Brynn tried to think. "Most of Jacob's disapproval was directed at me. As far as I can remember, he never even *met* my mom. And look, if he had a problem with Cortexia, and if he tried to talk to me about it, I would have told my mom, and she would have listened."

"You're being a little naïve."

Brynn's hackles went up. "What makes you say that?"

"I just mean . . ." Dex's gaze wandered over to the kids playing pinball again. "Cortexia is going to make your family a lot of money. Your mom wouldn't have to work anymore if she didn't want to."

"Of course she's going to want to—"

Dex held up his hand. "That's not my point. If Cortexia goes on the market and your mom earns money from the patent royalties, your life is going to change. You could go to any college you wanted. Your family could buy a bigger house—lots of bigger houses. That kind of money is enticing for anyone. It can open a lot of doors. But if a blip came up in the clinical trials . . . well, there was so much hype about Cortexia already, it might have been easier just to bury it."

Brynn gaped. "Are you seriously saying that my mom hid information about Cortexia because she's dying to get rich?"

"I'm only saying—"

She shot to her feet. "Just days ago, you cared about my mom. You cared about *me*. But now you think we're criminals. I'm a terrorist, she's a greedy murderer. Thanks for the benefit of the doubt."

She snaked through the café and stormed out the front door. The chilly air assaulted her, and she squinted in the bright sunshine. She felt so angry . . . and so confused. What if Dex was *right*? Was it possible? Her mom had hidden something huge from her, and Brynn was positive she would never have told her if her dad hadn't considered it a "teachable moment." She'd looked so pissed when Brynn's dad forced it out of her! And then her first reaction was asking Brynn not to spill the beans at the Cortexia launch? Who *was* this woman, and what had she done with Brynn's hero?

Maybe there *was* something wrong with Cortexia that her mom had let slip through the cracks. Maybe she *had* gotten caught up in the lure and seduction of the money, in the same way, years ago, she'd gotten caught up in succeeding at Harvard. Brynn thought about the panic that went through her household when the water heater stopped working, or when they needed repairs on their roof, or when the permission slips came around for a summer class trip to Europe that cost three thousand dollars. And now college was coming up. If looking the other way promised to put an extra lump of cash in her bank account, maybe her mom had gone for it.

Dr. Caldwell had mentioned how unprecedented it was that Cortexia had been approved so quickly by the FDA. That meant they must have falsified the data in the trials legitimately enough to fool the review team . . . or maybe they had a review team on their payroll. Maybe certain crooked FDA officials also stood to make a profit from the medication.

But could Brynn really believe her mom would allow that? She shut her eyes. The mother *she* knew was the type of person who went back into the grocery store to pay for a twelve-pack of soda on the bottom of her cart that the checkout person had forgotten to scan. The mother *she* knew didn't even cheat at Monopoly.

But she cheated at Harvard, came a small, teasing voice in her head. *And then she erased the evidence.*

"Brynn." Dex stopped her before she could cross the street. Two bright spots had appeared on his cheeks, and his eyes were full of sadness. "I'm sorry. I shouldn't have made that assumption about your mom. Okay? But at the same time, we have to consider all the options of why you joined this group, and who they are, why things got this far, and how to stop it."

Brynn grumbled under her breath, trying to steady her emotions. "Okay. But let's not say anything we'll regret until we know for sure. Deal?"

"Deal." Dex shoved his hands into his pockets and stared at the traffic. "So what do you want to do next? How can we figure out who these ACL people are?"

"I don't know. I've already tried to write to the people texting me, asking for more information, but every time I do, they just say I already know everything and that I should stop asking questions."

"Can I see the texts they sent you?"

Brynn nodded and pulled out her phone. Dex stepped away from the curb and into an alleyway, cupping his hand around the screen. He called up a website and started to tap the keyboard. "We might be able to triangulate the location of the phone that sent those texts," he murmured, dragging the offending texts into a browser window.

Brynn blinked. "How'd you know how to do *that*?"

"Because I interned with the NSA, remember?" He

frowned when a new window came up. "Should have known. Your ACL texts were spoof-sent."

"Spoof what?"

"Whoever sent you these used a website that anonymously sends the text from a fake number. People do that when they don't want you to trace them." He sighed, sounding disappointed. "Maybe we search for backlash against Cortexia online?" His fingers started to fly on his own phone. "Usually people who have issues with medications that are about to come out on the market congregate on Reddit or a similar forum. Maybe *those* are the people behind ACL."

Brynn trolled for the same thing, but she frowned at the Google results. "I'm not getting anything at all. Every Cortexia post is positive."

Dex clicked his teeth together. "But could that be a clue? Maybe someone took all the negative stuff down."

Brynn scoffed. "Still, that doesn't get us any closer to figuring out who ACL is—or how we can find them."

"You looked into the gray Toyota?" Dex tried hopefully.

"I've looked into *everything.*"

They sat back and stared at each other blankly. Brynn felt stuck. And scared. Seven days wasn't much time to figure anything out. Maybe they *should* call the police. But if they did, what if she was dragged to jail? What if, instead of going to MIT, Brynn spent her late teens in prison?

Then she had another thought. One she wasn't fond of, but one they might need to pursue. "Maybe we can get a clue into who these protestors are by getting to the source of the problem."

"Which is?"

"We could go through my mom's office at BioXin. To see if there's anything wrong with Cortexia. *And* if BioXin is covering it up."

THIRTEEN

As Brynn and Dex pulled past a large sign on a hill that read BIOXIN in space-age lettering, a campus-like compound on thirty acres of prime Virginia farmland greeted them. The BioXin site boasted green lawns, walking paths, gazebos, tennis courts, a separate commissary building, a gym, and even a day care. Most of the activity took place at the main building, a monolithic structure jutting out of the trees up the hill. Swinging Dex's Jeep into the parking lot, they watched as employees swarmed in and out of the front doors, their mouths stretched into grins. On every other visit here, Brynn had found the BioXin workers chipper, efficient, energetic. But today, they looked sort of... stiff. Like robots.

Dex locked the car. "Are you ready?"

Brynn shrugged. *Not really,* she wanted to say. She started across the parking lot anyway, her shoulders thrown back. She could do this. She had to.

There was a large desk at the back of the huge atrium lobby for guests to check in. Brynn gave her name to the guard, trying her best to eliminate the hitch in her voice. Her hands trembled as she showed him her ID. As he printed out their passes, she glanced up at the atrium, a soaring space of marble, glass, fountains, and gardens. This was where the launch party would be. And maybe the bomb, too? Her stomach turned over.

Her mother's office was on the second floor. As they walked to the elevator, Dex tapped her arm. Brynn flinched; it was the first time he'd touched her since he'd seen the drawing of the bomb. "Are you *sure* your mom's in a meeting right now?"

"She's fastidious about keeping her calendar up-to-date. She won't be in her office."

They stepped inside an open elevator car. Before the doors closed, a large group crammed in with them. Some wore BioXin lab coats. One was a security guard with a gun on his belt. Brynn kept her eyes trained on her shoes, glad no one could hear how hard her heart was pounding.

The elevator dinged on two. The doors slid open, and Dex stepped out first, signaling for Brynn to follow. Her mother's lab, called Halcyon Industries, was at the end of the hall, through a large glass door. Dex found his way there easily. Brynn was grateful for his innate sense of direction, because right now, she felt completely lost.

She peered through the window to the office. The lab was visible past reception, though most of the stations and work areas were unoccupied. Just then, a group of at least ten people in suits swept through the lobby, deep in conversation. Brynn ducked down.

"Who are they?" Dex whispered.

"I don't know. Not lab people, that's for sure." She wished she'd see someone familiar, like Martin, her mother's assistant. These people looked like clones.

"Maybe they're from marketing, or corporate," Dex suggested. "They're probably having meetings about the launch." He looked at her. "Come on. Let's go in."

Dex pressed through the door. The receptionist eyed them cautiously. "Can I help you?"

Brynn swallowed nervously. "I'm Brynn Caldwell. Celeste Caldwell's daughter."

"Of course!" Brynn wasn't sure, but she thought the tiniest flutter of dismay seemed to pass across the receptionist's face. "Your mom is very busy right now," she said. "She has meetings all morning. Is this an emergency?"

"Not exactly," Brynn said, spitting out what she and Dex had rehearsed. "But I'm supposed to wait in her office until she's done."

The woman's eyes darted from Brynn to Dex, then back

to Brynn again. She seemed hesitant, but after a moment, she hit a button to unlock the door that led to the lab. "All right. Do you know where it is?"

Dex nodded eagerly. He grabbed Brynn's hand and pulled her through the heavy door and past the empty lab desks, equipment, and machinery to a secondary hallway along the side of the building. Brynn was about to ask how Dex knew where he was going when he stopped and looked both ways. "Am I going the right way?"

Brynn nodded and pointed to the very end office. DR. CELESTE CALDWELL, read a brass plate on the door. They stepped inside the small, cramped space. Books were stacked every which way on the bookshelves. A jumble of framed photographs sat on the desk. Three massive cream-colored filing cabinets stood like sentinels by the windows.

Dex shut the door softly behind them. "According to her calendar, how much time do we have?"

"About thirty minutes." Brynn's gaze fell on something across the room. On one of the bookshelves, next to her mother's dog-eared textbooks, bound reports, and stacks of research, was a framed drawing of the different layers of the earth's crust Brynn had made in second grade. Tucked into the corner of that was Brynn's school picture from last year. Two shelves down stood a framed card Brynn had drawn for her mom for Mother's Day when she was nine. Above it was a snapshot of Brynn from last February. She stood behind a podium, grinning broadly because she'd gotten the last question in ChemE Jeopardy correct.

A lump formed in Brynn's throat. Could she really not trust someone who loved her so much? She shut her eyes, trying to snap out of it. They had to get to work.

She trudged over to one of the cabinets. She opened it slowly, daunted by all the file folders. Most of them were labeled with phrases she didn't understand. She pulled out one and glanced at the papers inside. The first sheet was some sort of chemical test, but Brynn couldn't tell for what. She dropped it back into the folder. It didn't seem to have anything to do with Cortexia.

Dex opened a drawer and began leafing through, too. Brynn peeked at his handsome profile, wishing her eyes could linger there, but she no longer felt like it was allowed. Ever since he'd seen the bomb schematic, Dex had been so shut off. Unaffectionate. She wasn't even sure if they *were* a couple anymore.

"Are you finding anything?" she asked after a few minutes.

"Nah," he answered. "Honestly, most of this I don't even understand."

"Me neither." Brynn cleared her throat. "So, I emailed Jacob." She tried to sound casual.

Dex looked up sharply. *"Why?"*

"I wanted to know if he's the one who's been getting in touch with me, sending me those texts."

Dex slammed the drawer shut a little too forcefully. "You

still have his email address? I thought you said you erased all that after you realized how toxic he was."

"I'm not going to get back together with him," she said, deciding to ignore his question. "There's no need for you to be jealous."

"I'm not jealous." Dex sounded disgusted.

"Anyway, he hasn't written me back," Brynn mumbled despondently. "I can't figure out why he would protest Cortexia. It doesn't make sense."

"You should have run it by me before you did something like that."

"Oh, *should* I have?" Brynn snapped, suddenly livid. "I can't make my own decisions?"

They stared at each other. The wall clock ticked noisily. Dex was the first to look away. "Sorry, sorry. I just . . . It's hard hearing that guy's name. But I see your point. I get why you contacted him."

They fell into tense silence. Brynn pulled out another piece of paper. It was printed with numbers she didn't understand. It also had several signatures on it, as though various people had signed off on the results.

"Hey," Dex called from his cabinet. His voice was grudging. "This might be something."

He held a printout of an email chain titled *Clinical, Cortexia.*

Brynn frowned at it. "This is dated only a year ago—but that's impossible. My mom said the trials were over by then."

"Maybe they kept a few trials open because they didn't trust something about the drug?" Dex posited.

"Maybe." Brynn's eyes narrowed at the numbers in the email. "And if we can figure out *why*—"

"Excuse me?"

They whirled around. The piece of paper slid from Dex's hands to the floor, but he didn't stoop to pick it up.

Standing in the doorway was Dr. Lowell, Brynn's mom's partner.

Busted.

FOURTEEN

D r. Lowell strode into the office. "Brynn." He had a pleasant enough voice, but his posture was rigid. "Does your mother know you're here?"

Out the window, Brynn heard a series of sirens, and she concentrated on them for a moment, trying to gather her thoughts. "Not exactly," she said finally. "But I have a permission slip I'm supposed to get signed for school, and my mom brought it with her to work by mistake. She said it's on her desk, but I'm afraid it got mixed in with her papers and she filed it away or something." She let out a goofy little laugh, as if to say, *We silly scientists! Always misplacing things!*

Dr. Lowell crossed his arms over his chest, looking like

he didn't believe her. Brynn readied for him to read her the riot act, but then he turned. "I'll be back." He hurried out of the office.

She turned to Dex. "We have to get out of here."

"No!" Dex whispered. "That will make us look even guiltier! And anyway, I'm not leaving until I figure out what this means." He picked up the incriminating email and pushed it toward Brynn again. She studied it, hoping to see a crack in Cortexia's foundation, but all it said was that they were going to continue tracking Cortexia's test patients by the unique numbers that corresponded to their birthdays. *Sounds good*, Brynn's mother had replied. Brynn felt her stomach twist. So her mom *did* know about Cortexia still being in trials last year.

"Why was Cortexia still in trials?" Dex whispered. "Do you think they caught something that was wrong and wanted to test for it? Or maybe run another trial, fudge the numbers, and show *that* to the FDA, saying the drug is safe?"

"Dex, we don't have time for this!" Brynn shoved the email back into a drawer. "Lowell is probably getting security. We have to leave." She closed the cabinet tight.

But as they were heading into the hall, Brynn collided with Lowell's tall, skinny frame.

"Oof," the scientist said, staggering backward a little, his glasses slipping down his nose. He peered at them with annoyance. "Where are you going? I told you I'd be right back."

Brynn flinched. "Uh, we don't want to take up your time. We know you're busy."

Lowell glanced over his shoulder. The hallway was empty. Then he leaned so close to Brynn his mouth nearly grazed her ear. "Third drawer down," he murmured almost inaudibly. "Filed under *X*."

Brynn started. "What?"

"Filed under *X*. It's all in there."

His face gave nothing away. He reminded Brynn of one of those ventriloquists who could throw his voice without moving his mouth. If she'd been standing even a few feet away, she wouldn't have believed that he'd been the one speaking.

In the tiniest gesture, Lowell flicked his head back toward her mother's office, as if to say, *Go back there. I'll keep watch.* Brynn slowly backpedaled into the office. Dex did, too. Lowell quietly shut the door on them. Once he was gone, Brynn and Dex stared at each other.

"What the hell was that?" Dex breathed.

"I—I don't know," Brynn said.

Brynn turned to the third filing cabinet drawer from the top. The drawer made an earsplitting screech as she opened it. At the very back was a file marked *X*, just as Lowell predicted. She pulled out a thick folder. The pages were all ruffled and creased, as though they might have been fished out of the trash. On the first page were the words *Clinical Trial Results*, but this one was dated two years ago, not one.

Brynn's heart squeezed. What was this? Did she really want to see it?

"Whoa," Dex whispered, riffling through the file. A few pages in were smaller, index-card-sized papers, with BioXin's logo at the top. A line at the top read *Patient ID Number*, and each card was printed with a unique set of digits—perhaps the birthday identifiers that had been discussed in the email they'd found earlier. Below the patient IDs was information on the trial, like lists of the number of injections a patient had received and MRI and blood work results. But on some of the cards, black lines had been drawn through all of the data. Brynn squinted hard, but she couldn't tell what had been written under the ink. She looked down at her hands. They were shaking.

"Why would someone cross stuff out?" she whispered.

"Maybe it was bad news." Dex laid four cards on the desk. "And look—there seems to be a unifying factor for which patients' data was erased. If the patients' IDs are their birthdays, all these patients were born in the early 2000s. Meaning they're teenagers."

Brynn stepped back. "There were no trials for teenagers."

"Are you sure?" Dex kept flipping through cards, pulling more and more with inked-out data. It was true: According to their birthday IDs, they'd all been in their teens when the trials had taken place. "Kids go through trauma just like adults. Maybe a clinical trial was made available."

"But my mom controlled all the trials. They were always on soldiers. Never kids."

"Perhaps this is what you learned about," Dex said. "Maybe this is why you joined ACL."

"But if the ACL people knew this, if they knew data was being erased, why didn't they go public?" Brynn was thoroughly puzzled. "Why did they go straight to building a bomb?"

"Maybe they only know generalities, not specifics." Dex tapped the top of the folder. "Maybe what they need is in this file. Or maybe they tried to tell someone, but whoever it was didn't listen. So they needed to up the ante."

Brynn peered into the hallway. Across the hall was an empty treatment room, probably used during Cortexia trials. The door was ajar, and she could see part of a reclined, padded examination chair, covered in sterile paper. She turned back to Dex. "I need to tell my mom about this. Now."

Dex caught her arm. "Wait, Brynn. *No.*"

"Why not?" Brynn wriggled away. "She needs to see this. She needs to know if there's something wrong with the drug."

"But what if she already *knows*, Brynn? This stuff is in her office."

Brynn froze. Her mom's confession about what she'd done at Harvard swam back to her . . . but so did the look of grief and regret on her mom's face. She glanced at the family pictures on the bookshelf again. *Unbelievable.* It went to show you couldn't trust anyone.

Brynn scooped up the folder and marched into the corridor.

"Brynn." Dex chased after her. He caught up to her just as a stream of people exited a nearby conference room. Brynn stopped in her tracks, surprised by all the faces. Then she spied her mother, second to last out the door. Dr. Caldwell was in midsentence with one of her colleagues, but she stopped when she noticed her daughter. For a brief second, Dr. Caldwell looked shocked ... and then almost like she wanted to run. But maybe Brynn was seeing things, because a moment later, she was striding toward them, a big forced smile on her face.

"Well, hey!" Dr. Caldwell sounded friendly enough, but a muscle in her cheek was twitching, something that always happened when she was angry. "What are you two doing here?"

"Mom," Brynn began. She glanced around for Dr. Lowell, but she didn't see him anywhere. *Just say it,* she willed herself. *Spit it out.* But she couldn't. There were too many people around. And she was unnerved by that look she'd just seen on her mom's face. She hid the folder behind her back.

Dr. Caldwell stepped closer. "Perhaps you're here to apologize," she said in a low, dangerous voice.

Brynn felt a shiver down her spine. *She* didn't need to

apologize for anything. Then again, it was a good excuse. "Yeah, something like that," she murmured. "Sorry."

"Thank you," Dr. Caldwell said primly. "I appreciate it."

She pulled Brynn into a hug, but her arms were rigid. Brynn stood stiffly for the hug, keeping the folder hidden behind her. Unlike Dex's warm brush of skin, her mom's fingers were ice-cold. As she pulled away, she seemed so different. Unfamiliar. Her eyes were keener, more cunning, and much more aware. She seemed to give off an air of distance—even of watchful danger.

It felt like Brynn's heart was breaking into a zillion pieces.

Her mom's cell phone rang, breaking the crackling awkwardness. Dr. Caldwell checked the screen, then gave Brynn and Dex one last loaded glance. "It's nice to see you guys, but I'm awfully busy with the launch. This isn't a good time."

"Got it," Brynn snapped. And without even giving her mother a wave, she turned on her heel and walked as calmly as she could to the door to the elevator. Only after she'd stabbed the Down button did she glance back into the lab. Dr. Caldwell hadn't moved from outside the conference room. There was a look on her face that was very far from happy. Her gaze hadn't moved from Brynn's back.

The elevator pinged. Brynn hurried inside with Dex, then collapsed against the far wall and put her hands over her face. "So *that* just happened."

"Your mom seemed . . . weird." Dex glanced at the folder in Brynn's hand. "I don't blame you for not saying anything."

Brynn held the folder tightly to her chest. It felt so precious suddenly, as though she were cradling a baby. She glanced at the page on top. It was another list of patients, some with black lines drawn through their results. Then she noticed one of the patient IDs at the bottom. A few had been penned in blue ink, almost like an afterthought. One read *022900*. There were no results after it, just the number. Brynn's skin prickled. That was a coincidence of a birthday. Leap Day 2000. It was *her* birthday.

It was like someone had struck a match in her mind. Hazy light illuminated a scene, and suddenly she was somewhere else. Strapped to a chair—a reclined, padded chair she'd seen recently, in fact. And there was that man again, the one hidden behind a cheap surgical mask. *How much do you know?* he demanded.

Brynn thrashed. *I don't know what you're talking about.*

The man grew enraged. *Are you going to try to stop us?* That was new, something Brynn hadn't remembered before.

What you're doing isn't right, Brynn heard herself answer. This was new, too.

What's your plan?

Brynn let out a groan. Tears were running down her cheeks.

Who are they, anyway?

Brynn shook her head. *I can't tell you that.*

The man glanced at someone out of view. *We need to do this,* he growled. *We have no choice.*

And then another face emerged—someone else in a mask. He unzipped something from a small, elliptical pouch that bore a familiar logo. Inside was a syringe with a long sharp point. As he held it to the light, its tip gleamed with a drop of liquid. Brynn's eyes widened. *No!* she screamed, but the man didn't listen. He plunged it into the meat of Brynn's biceps. She yelped.

Stop squirming, he said.

But Brynn didn't stop. She thrashed as the liquid entered her bloodstream. She felt the breath leave her body. Even as she lost consciousness, she still tried to kick her legs, desperate to ruin these people, desperate to make them pay.

"Brynn!"

She opened her eyes. She was crouched in the corner of the elevator, her arms wrapped around her knees. Dex stood over her, his face a knot of concern. "Are you all right? You just . . . *disappeared.*"

The memory swirled around Brynn like dark smoke. The light shining into her eyes. The anger in that man's voice. And that chair—it looked just like the chair in her mom's lab. Those people in that vision weren't part of ACL—they were part of something else. She could feel it. They were people who wanted something different, people she should fear even more.

Her mind took a turn, and she saw the needle heading for her arm again. Struggling hard, using every bit of brainpower she could, she scratched and clawed to hold on to the memory before it faded. The label on the little pouch that held the syringe swam into view, and she gasped. She looked at Dex in horror.

"What?" Dex cried.

"I—I remembered something else," Brynn stammered. "I think I was given Cortexia."

FIFTEEN

"Oh my God." Brynn pressed her hands against her head. "Oh my *God*."

It crashed back to her tumultuously, a wave breaking against a rocky shore. Her body bucked against the Cortexia injection, then went slack. The men cackled above her, murmuring that the problem was now solved. The same pair of strong arms that had brought her here lifted her again, tied a blindfold around her head, and carried her away. But this time, Brynn lay limply in the man's arms, not even struggling when he tossed her back into the trunk.

When she awoke, she was lying in her bed with a massive headache. It was unclear how she'd gotten there. She had no knowledge of what had happened before; it felt like someone had ripped a page from her memory. Out the window, the sun sizzled in the sky. Brynn had stared at it, feeling dull and blank. She felt . . . *empty*, her mind scooped of every pertinent thought.

And that's because it was. That's how Cortexia worked.

"Brynn," Dex was saying to her, "let's get out of here. Come on."

The elevator was standing open in the lobby. People were beginning to stare at them curiously. Brynn struggled to her feet, studying BioXin's nucleus-like logo on the far back wall. It was just like the one she'd seen on the pouch that contained the syringe. Dex was right. If she didn't get out of here right now, she was going to freak.

Dex pulled her outside, across the campus, and back to his car. But it was parked so far away, past lines and lines of vehicles packed closely together. The parking lot was eerily empty at this hour, and the sun was angled such that it cast no shadows across the concrete.

"I can't believe it," Brynn said after a few moments. "I was given Cortexia. I'm right here in the test results."

"You were in a clinical trial?" Dex was aghast.

"I don't think so. Someone gave it to me after grilling me about what I knew—it's from that same memory that came back to me in the cemetery. So I'm not sure how my information wound up on this page." She pointed to her birth date on the paper. "It's penned in at the bottom, and I have no lab results. I'm not sure I was an official patient.

That probably means I never saw a psychologist, either. I definitely don't *remember* seeing a psychologist—only my family doctor, who gave me meds for my depression." Her throat felt tight. "What happens to a patient if they're given Cortexia by force but then don't talk to a therapist? If you're in such a suggestive state, could whoever forced it on you convince you of anything they wanted?"

"That's a scary idea," Dex said. "But back up a sec. Why would ACL inject you with Cortexia if they were fighting against it?"

Brynn stared back at the BioXin building. With its blocky facade, it looked like a prison, and the bright sun glared across its black-tinted windows. "I'm not sure the people who injected me *were* part of ACL. In fact, I think they were fighting against ACL." She repeated what the man in her memory had said: *Are you going to try to stop us?* And how she'd responded: *What you're doing isn't right.*

"Couldn't you have been referring to the bomb?" Dex asked, peering down a new row, searching for his car.

"Maybe. But it feels like whatever he was doing was even *worse* than a bomb."

Dex sniffed. "What's worse than a bomb?"

"I wish I knew." A leaden feeling had settled in her stomach. How had that guy in the surgical mask gotten his hands on Cortexia, anyway? As far as she knew, her mother's lab kept the precious medication under lock and key.

She looked up at Dex, feeling the blood drain from her face. "What if those men work in my mom's lab?"

Dex didn't look surprised. "It could make sense. BioXin might have been trying to shut you up about what you found out was wrong with Cortexia. The thing your mom might have known about."

Brynn felt uneasy. "You think my *mom's* in on this?"

"Don't you?" Dex chewed on his bottom lip. "It's not like we can trust her right now. We don't know what she's capable of."

Brynn swallowed hard. She supposed that was true.

"You really can't remember what you found out?" Dex asked.

Brynn shook her head miserably. "It's all gone." She gasped. "This could explain why there's so much I can't remember from this summer! I always chalked it up to depression . . . but what if it was from the Cortexia injection instead? Receiving those injections, being in a suggestive state—what if someone *forced* me to forget whatever was happening to me?"

Dex looked spooked. "God, Brynn. That's . . . *horrible*. I'm so sorry." He took her hands. "Forget what I said about figuring this out within twenty-four hours. I won't turn you in. You didn't know what was happening to you. I get that now, for real."

There was a huge lump in her throat. "Thanks," she said

softly, sadly. It felt good that Dex was on her side again, but she hated the circumstances. And then a monstrous thought hit her. She held up the folder. "Wait. There's no data about me in these files, just my birth date. But if we're right that Cortexia affects teenage patients differently than it does adults, causing results they had to *cross out*, then that means I might be—"

Her throat caught. She stopped short and stared at her arms, half expecting them to break into reactionary hives, or for a third hand to grow out of her wrist, or for her body to suddenly convulse. It was even scarier not knowing what the side effects were; they could be *anything*.

Something else occurred to her. "What if some of these other patients were in ACL, too?" She pointed at the birth dates penned in under hers. "There's no data for these patients, either. Maybe they were just like me. Maybe BioXin—*my mom*—was injecting them just to shut them up."

"You might be on to something," Dex said.

Together, they stared at the pages. Brynn scanned the penned-in birth dates to see if she recognized any of them. Could one of these numbers offer a clue to the people who were texting her? It made her sick to think of her mother selecting other people. It made her sick to consider her mother was involved at *all*. But Dex was right: Signs were pointing in that direction. All at once, she was relieved she hadn't said anything to her mom in the office a few minutes ago. Who was to say her mom wouldn't have grabbed Brynn and injected her all over again, right then?

Suddenly, Dex looked up. His eyes focused on something behind them in the parking lot. He drew up to his full height. "Hey—" Brynn heard him say, when suddenly she felt a sharp *crack* on the back of her skull.

Blood pooled in her mouth. She landed on her side and squealed in pain. She lay there writhing, catching quick flashes of someone in a white coat above her. *"You have to stop,"* a voice warned.

Her eyes flew open. Dex was on the ground, too, moaning and clutching his groin. "Dex!" she cried, crawling to him. Footsteps rang out behind her, and she turned and squinted. The parking lot was empty. The attacker was gone.

She turned back to Dex. His eyes were squeezed closed, and his breath came out in puffs. "Are you all right?" she cried.

"Yeah," Dex heaved. "I think so."

"What happened?" Brynn asked.

He sat up, still puffing. "Someone came out of nowhere. They hit you, then me."

"Who?"

"I couldn't really see. It was too fast. Some guy in a white coat."

That was what Brynn remembered, too. "A scientist?" she whispered.

Then Dex looked around, panic crossing his features. "Shit." He patted the concrete. "Brynn. He took the folder."

Brynn's stomach sank. Her mind drifted back to her mom coming out of that meeting. Her mother's eyes had flicked to Brynn's hands quickly, then looked away. Goose bumps rose on her skin.

Beep.

She jumped. She scrambled for her cell phone, wincing at the way the sudden movement made her aching head swim. There was a new text on the screen. *Nice to see you today, honey,* her mom wrote. *But we need to talk, and we both know it. Meet me for dinner at Newick's at 7.*

The blood drained from her cheeks. She showed the text to Dex. "What should I do?" she whispered. All of a sudden, her mom felt like a stranger to her. A *dangerous* one.

Dex's lips trembled. "I guess you meet her for dinner."

DON'T PANIC, **BRYNN** told herself. She stood in front of Newick's, a little diner tucked into a back inlet of the Chesapeake and famous for the best crab cakes in all of Annapolis. Golden light glowed from inside, and a classic-rock song lilted from the speakers. This was where her family came for celebrations—like when her mom had the lab breakthrough with Cortexia, or when they found out it would be launched to the public. But Brynn wasn't feeling celebratory today.

Don't panic, she repeated to herself. She remembered the instructions Dex had given her. *Play it cool. But don't trust anything she says.* When she saw her mother sitting at their usual back table, her stomach tightened. Her mom had forgotten to take off her lab coat, though Brynn wondered if it wasn't absentmindedness but a calculated message. The person who'd grabbed that file back from them today wore a lab coat. Was he from BioXin? Maybe even her mother's specific lab?

She should leave, she thought. She should get out of here and try to figure out what to do. But then her mother looked up and noticed Brynn in the doorway. She smiled weakly and waved.

Brynn tried to smile back. She had no choice but to make her way over to the table. She slid into a seat and undid her napkin, afraid to make eye contact. "Hey. Did you already order?"

Dr. Caldwell leaned across the table and gave Brynn a kiss on her cheek. The sensation of her lips lingered on Brynn's skin like a burn. "I got you the mushroom burger," she said, sounding a little tentative. "Is that okay?"

"Uh-huh." Brynn ached at how ordinary everything seemed. A mushroom burger was what she always ordered here. And her mom was drinking a sparkling water with lime, something she always drank. How was she going to get through this? So many questions bounced in her mind. What did her mother know? Had she been there in the lab the day Brynn was injected? How could she allow such a thing?

"So listen." Her mother laced her fingers together. "We have something important to talk about."

Brynn's heart stopped. Her mother wasn't beating around the bush.

Dr. Caldwell sat back, her gaze still intense. Brynn held her breath.

"Do you think it's bad luck to wear black to the launch?" her mom asked.

Brynn blinked, caught off guard. "What?"

"I found this black dress at Saks, and I really love it." Dr. Caldwell fiddled with her straw. "But black seems so . . . funereal. I don't want to send the wrong message."

Brynn's throat felt dry. She unwrapped her silverware from the napkin to forestall a response. "You seriously brought me here to talk about your *outfit*?" she muttered, hearing the acid in her voice.

Dr. Caldwell stiffened. "Fine. I didn't bring you here to talk about that. I was just trying to be nice. But clearly, you don't give a crap."

Brynn flinched. Her mom's voice was sharp, determined. Her eyes met Brynn's again, but Brynn looked down fast. Her heart started to pound.

"I need you to straighten up, Brynn," Dr. Caldwell said, her tone menacing. "You've been very unsupportive lately, and I don't know where it's coming from. I need you to be on our team through this Cortexia launch, is that clear? And you need to drop the attitude."

Fury rose inside her. "Are you kidding me?"

Her mother's mouth was taut. "No, I'm not. And I'm the mother, not you. So you need to listen."

Brynn put her palms flat on the table. "Has it occurred to you this attitude is because I have no idea who you are anymore?"

Her mother looked exasperated. "This is about the Harvard incident? You're *that* angry about it?"

"Of course not!" Brynn tried to remain calm. "It's about how you're a fraud, Mom! It's about how Cortexia isn't the wonder drug it seems, and it's all just about the profits, and you've known that all along!"

"*What?*" Dr. Caldwell looked shocked. She moved closer to Brynn, glancing around nervously to see if anyone was listening. "What are you talking about?"

Brynn crossed her arms over her chest. "You know what I'm talking about."

Dr. Caldwell stared at her in horror. "Just because I lied at Harvard over twenty-five years ago doesn't mean I've lied about anything having to do with Cortexia. Lives are at stake here."

"They certainly are," Brynn muttered bitterly.

Dr. Caldwell recoiled. "I would never do anything dishonest with Cortexia. I would never put profit over people's health, and I can't believe you'd ever think that about me."

Brynn stared at her mother. Dex's voice rang in her ears. *Don't trust a word she says.*

"Here we go!" the waiter interrupted, making Brynn jump as he set down their meals. Steam rose from both the plates. "Enjoy!"

The silence curled around them as he walked away. Brynn stared at her burger; she couldn't fathom taking a single bite. She wanted to run out of here. Run far, far away.

But she couldn't do that. She couldn't just sit idly by and let BioXin distribute Cortexia to the general public. Nor could she sit back and let ACL bomb the launch. *Everything* depended on her... and she still had no answers. She had to find out more—about *everything*. If only some of those birth dates had jogged her memory. If only the person on the other end of the text messages would write back. Brynn had sent another text to the jumble of numbers on her way here, saying she now knew what Cortexia did to teens, but that they had to fill her in on more because she'd been *given* Cortexia, too. But she'd received no reply. It was like the person on the other end of the texts had fulfilled his duty and backed off. The bombing was happening, Brynn had remembered enough, the task had been completed. And she was just culpable enough *not* to automatically call the cops.

Then she thought about her email inbox. She hadn't

checked it since this morning. Under the table, she refreshed her account, but Jacob still hadn't replied. Suddenly, another folder caught her eye. *Junk Mail.* She clicked on it, her heart pounding. Sure enough, a reply from Jacob's email address had come through. Brynn could hardly believe her eyes.

> Stop bothering me. We're not getting back
> together. Totally happy here in CO. Dating two
> hot girls at once. So again—we're done. Got it?

Just reading the words, Brynn could hear his irate tone. She tried to picture his face, but saw only that sneer. She felt indignant. *I HAVE A BOYFRIEND, TOO!* she wanted to type back. *And he's much, much better than you!* The rage boiled inside her, but she didn't allow herself to get wrapped up in the rejection. Okay, so Jacob wasn't the bomber. So who had convinced her to join ACL? Her dad? That seemed unlikely—he was so supportive of Cortexia. Her mother's assistant, Martin? He hardly seemed the type.

Lowell? Brynn recalled the words he'd murmured in the lab. He'd led them right to those important files—he *wanted* them to be found. Of course!

But suddenly she was seized with horror. Mild-mannered Lowell, who bird-watched on the weekends and was really into model trains, building a *bomb*? It seemed so unthinkable.

Unless whatever was wrong with Cortexia was so horrific, so devastating, it had driven him mad. . . .

Brynn leapt to her feet, suddenly desperate to reach him. Her mother glanced over her water glass. "Where are you going?"

"I'm done." And with that, Brynn bolted out the front door and sprinted down the dead-end street. She checked over her shoulder; her mother wasn't coming after her. *Shit,* she thought. *Shit, shit, shit.* She'd shown her hand in there. She'd told her mom that she knew. But did her mom really expect to get away with this? Did she think she could fool people, even her own daughter? She hadn't even *gotten* to that part of the accusation yet—that her mother had used *Brynn* as a guinea pig in whatever psychotic experiment she was trying to cover up.

Would her mother get her minions after her for this? Would they forcibly inject her with Cortexia all over again, beating the memories from her?

The next street over boasted a 7-Eleven, some small homes, and an apartment complex. Brynn looped around the 7-Eleven and crouched against the wall farthest from Newick's, then pulled out her phone and brought up BioXin's website. After a few taps, she was able to find Halcyon Industry's section of the site. But when she clicked on "Directory," only a main number came up. Nothing else.

Frustrated, she dialed the line, hoping that either a

receptionist would still be there or the voice mail system would offer an extension directory. The phone rang twice, three times, then four. A voice mail picked up, but it was for a general mailbox, and it only let callers leave a message.

Brynn let out a frustrated sigh. Now what? She knew where Lowell lived—they'd visited his family's house in Georgetown a few times—but showing up there seemed risky, and it was doubtful he'd tell her the truth about being a Unabomber in front of his whole family. No, she had to ambush him somewhere alone. Not at the lab—she was too much of a target there. Somewhere else.

An idea struck her. Fingers flying, she texted her mother's lab assistant. *I'm planning a surprise dinner for my mom for all the awesome stuff she has going on, but I need to know her schedule,* she wrote. *Does she have any events coming up before the launch? Any other interviews? I just don't want to plan it on a day when she already has something scheduled.* If Rainer Wilson wanted to interview Brynn's mother and Lowell together, it probably meant another journalist would, too.

Martin wrote back quickly. *Well, Monday's the investors' dinner. Huge deal.*

Gotcha, Brynn typed, her mind galloping. *Is the whole company going?*

Nah, just her and Lowell and some execs. I get to sit that out! Martin added a smiling emoji. Brynn replied with a thumbs-up emoji. Martin wrote back again asking how she was holding up before the launch—was it crazy at home? Was she excited?

But Brynn's thoughts were far, far away. She needed to get to that investors' dinner. She needed to talk to Lowell, and find out everything, and stop the bomb.

No matter what.

SIXTEEN

FOUR DAYS TO LAUNCH

On Monday night, Brynn's hands shook as she did up the buttons of the unfamiliar white oxford shirt. "Help," she whispered to Dex, knowing there was no way she could tie the black tie properly. He leaned over and cinched it for her, then stood back. "You look good. Certainly the sexiest caterer I've ever seen."

Brynn gave him a wary nudge. "I want to blend in, not be sexy." Then she smiled. "You, however, look amazing."

They were crowded into a tiny bathroom in the lobby of the Four Seasons, where the BioXin investors' dinner was taking place. Earlier, they'd snuck around the back entrance to the hotel, and Brynn had managed to intercept two of the caterers, a blond girl about her size named Maddy, and a guy about Dex's size named West. Getting Maddy and West to hand over their uniforms and let Brynn and Dex take their places had cost Brynn all of the two hundred dollars in babysitting money she'd saved, but she needed to go incognito tonight. As Maddy the caterer, she'd be able to glide around the event unnoticed—and get to Lowell. Dex would provide backup in case she needed it.

"Are you sure you want to do this?" Dex asked as he helped her put on her jacket. "It's not like we're sure Lowell is part of ACL."

"It has to be him," Brynn said. "I've gone over every other possibility. We're running out of time, Dex. Why else would Lowell have passed us that secret folder?"

Dex peered out the bathroom door into the lobby. "It looks like everyone is going in. Just keep cool, okay? I'll be right behind you."

Brynn nodded and tried to smile, but her stomach was jumping all over the place. She adjusted her black wig, put on the thick, clear-lensed glasses she'd picked up at CVS, and pushed out through the bathroom door.

The lobby was crowded with people in suits and women in dresses. Most of them looked distinguished and important, and everyone was too busy schmoozing to notice Brynn as she hurried toward the kitchen. Her gaze flicked to the front drive, where valets were rushing around trying to park all the cars. A bell rang, and the guests began to file into the ballroom. Dex squeezed Brynn's shoulder. "Good luck."

"You, too."

Brynn strode into the kitchen as calmly as she could. Cooks manned countless stoves, frying, flipping, and sautéing. A prep line arranged and dressed salads. A woman who looked like the boss scanned the caterers. Brynn put her head down and avoided eye contact, not wanting the woman to scrutinize her. The servers were lining up to take out trays of salad, and Brynn huddled at the back.

"Table one," the boss instructed a server as she went out the door. "Table seven," she told another. She smiled at Dex, clearly finding him cute. "Table two." Then she got to Brynn. "Table three," she said, hefting a tray into her arms.

Brynn nodded and hurried into the ballroom, which was packed and humid. She didn't know where table three was, though mercifully there were place cards at the center of each table as a guide. Most of the guests had already sat down, and Brynn caught sight of her mom settling in at the very table she was supposed to deliver the salads to. She sucked in a breath. What if her mom noticed her under the glasses and wig? Could she really do this undercover?

She ducked her head, approached table three, and started passing out the salads, first to a few people from BioXin corporate she'd seen in the office the other day, and then to Dr. Kelley, one of her mother's colleagues. To her relief, everyone was so deep in conversation they barely noticed Brynn's presence. Practically tossing the salad at her mom's seat, Brynn dashed into the kitchen again. But before she turned, a familiar figure in the front doorway caught her eye. A tall, dashing man in a black suit was stepping into the ballroom. It was Senator Merriweather.

What was *he* doing here?

"Don't just stand there," a voice hissed in Brynn's ear. She whirled around to find another caterer, also with an empty tray, trying to get around her into the kitchen. "There's a million other salads to get out," the girl murmured as Brynn stepped aside. "And I really don't want to be the one who does all the work *again.*"

Brynn scurried after the girl and grabbed another tray of salads. Safe beneath her tray, she returned to the ballroom and quickly found where the senator had ended up. He, too, had been seated at table three. To Brynn's surprise, he glided directly over to Brynn's mother and tapped her arm. Her mother broke into a smile as soon as she saw him, and he gave her a friendly, familiar embrace. Brynn stopped short. They *knew* each other? How positively icky.

"Whoa."

Suddenly, Dex was next to her, his gaze on Brynn's mother and the senator, too. "Whoa," he said again. "Did you have any idea they knew each other?"

Brynn shook her head. "So does this mean he's an investor?"

"Makes sense. Cortexia is right up his alley."

Brynn rolled her jaw. Merriweather supported all things defense; of course he would rally for a medication that helped soldiers not only get over their issues, but also *get back out there and fight the terrorists.* "I thought my mom believed Merriweather was a blowhard," she murmured. But tonight, the two of them looked thrilled with each other, like they were old friends.

"Hello?" the boss said as she swept through. And just like that, Dex and Brynn shot apart and delivered their salads.

Brynn made three more trips into the kitchen, refilled water, and picked up a few dropped napkins. She tried hard to eavesdrop, hoping she'd hear something about Cortexia's "issues" . . . but she didn't hear a single mention of Cortexia at all. Heading out a fourth time, she spied Dr. Lowell settling into his seat at table three. Unlike the other guests at the event, who were throwing back cocktails and mingling enthusiastically, Lowell was drinking water, his forehead crinkled with tension, and he spoke to no one. Brynn gripped the tray tighter. He was clearly conflicted about being here. Conflicted about *Cortexia.* Was he thinking about bombing everyone? Maybe he was having second thoughts?

This was her chance.

She edged up to table three, as close as she dared, then cleared her throat. After a moment, Lowell looked her way. Brynn gave him a small wave, praying he would recognize her in the glasses and wig. Lowell did a double take. His eyes widened.

I need to speak to you, Brynn mouthed. *It's important.*

Lowell's jaw twitched. He shook his head and turned away. Brynn bit down on her lip, waiting for him to look at her again. His focus remained fixed on his salad plate.

Suddenly, she felt another pair of eyes on her. She peered around the room, her skin prickling. People were deep in conversation. Men stood and shook hands. Two women took a selfie. How many people in this room were in on Cortexia's secret? As investors, they all stood to gain if it went on the market. Did that mean they *all* knew?

She glanced toward Lowell again, willing him to look over. He calmly drank from his water glass, his back rigid. Another caterer approached him, holding a bottle of wine. Lowell shook his head and waved her away.

"We'll have more!" Brynn's mother trilled from across the table, gesturing for the bottle. The caterer circled around and poured wine into Dr. Caldwell's empty glass. The senator held his out for her to fill, too, giving Brynn's mother a wink. Brynn's stomach churned. Then she noticed that Dex was hovering close to them, maybe listening.

She trudged back to the kitchen, frustrated. The way Lowell was pointedly ignoring her wasn't something she'd anticipated. Could she follow him into the bathroom? Lure him outside somehow?

Dex returned to the kitchen, wiping at a wine stain on his white shirt.

"What was Merriweather saying to my mom?" Brynn asked him.

"I couldn't hear much, but it sounded like she was giving her spiel about Cortexia. The same one she gave on TV. Merriweather seemed pleased." Dex moved closer. "I also noticed your mom trying to catch Lowell's eye. He seems uncomfortable, right? Like something's bothering him?"

"I know," Brynn said, and she relayed how she'd tried to get Lowell's attention but he'd ignored her. "I guess I just have to try again," she said with determination.

"Go for it," Dex said. He frowned down at his shirt— the stain still hadn't come out. He squeezed Brynn's arm, then headed for the employee bathroom. A few caterers were heading out to collect empty salad plates, and Brynn fell in line with a tray. But as she walked down the hallway toward the ballroom, she felt a tug on the back of her jacket.

Suddenly, she was pulled into an alcove. The tray slipped from her hands. Two arms wrapped around her from behind, and she felt hot breath on her ear. *"Get out of here,"* said a voice.

"Huh?" Brynn wheeled around, desperate to know who was speaking to her.

"You're pushing your luck."

She felt hands around her neck. Her eyes rolled to the

back of her head, and her vision felt spotty. All of a sudden, she was sure she was going to pass out. In seconds, she slumped to the floor. Footsteps rang out in the hall—whoever had grabbed her was running away. Brynn wanted to get up, but she couldn't open her eyes. But then wires in her brain crossed, and a new pathway opened. Once again, Brynn was tied to that horrible chair. The man in the surgical mask stood over her. *Who are they?* he demanded, once again.

The Brynn in the memory looked away. *I can't tell you.*

There was more to the memory this time, like an extra door had opened up, showing her a new room. *Why not?* the same man exclaimed. *Don't you know they're dangerous? Don't you know* we're *the ones you should trust?*

Brynn trembled. *That's not true,* she'd said in an eggshell-thin voice.

He pulled out the Cortexia. As Brynn thrashed, someone in the back of the room let out a satisfied chuckle. And then there was the sound of a door slamming open. The man injecting Brynn raised his eyes toward it. *Hey,* a voice called out—a familiar voice, Brynn thought, but her mind was so jumbled, she couldn't figure out whose it was.

"Hey," someone said again. But the voice was different this time. Brynn opened her eyes. She was in the hall outside the ballroom once more. Someone stood above her, looking worried. "Maddy, are you okay?" she said.

Brynn's eyes adjusted. It was the boss of the catering company. The woman looked her over, and her kind expression shifted. "Wait, you're not Maddy," she said slowly. "Who are you?"

Brynn scrambled to her feet, realizing she'd been caught. "Um, I'm doing Maddy a favor. She asked me to fill in for the night."

The woman's nostrils flared. "I screen everyone here. She should have run this by me."

It was only then that Brynn realized how close they were to the ballroom. Though the music was still playing, quite a few of the guests were staring at them curiously. Brynn's gaze drifted to table three, but her mom was still deep in conversation with Merriweather. Dr. Lowell's seat was unoccupied, his napkin set neatly on his salad plate. Had she missed her chance? Where had he gone?

The catering boss's expression grew angrier and angrier. "I'm not paying someone I haven't vetted," she was saying. "Are you even properly trained as a caterer?"

"I—I'll go," Brynn stammered, quickly pulling off the jacket and moving away. "Please. I don't want any trouble. I'll go now."

Ignoring the woman's protest, Brynn hurried down the hall and burst through the back doors. *Help,* she texted Dex as soon as she stepped into the night. In moments, she heard footsteps. Dex burst through the door, still in uniform.

"Come on," he said, grabbing her arm and leading her to the Jeep. "What happened?" he asked as she slumped into the passenger seat and burst into tears.

Brynn just looked at him and shook her head. "A lot. And none of it good."

SEVENTEEN

THREE DAYS TO LAUNCH

On Tuesday evening, Brynn sat in the backseat of her mother's car as they pulled into the BioXin parking lot. Dr. Caldwell was talking a mile a minute, which she always did when she was nervous. They were returning to the BioXin building to make some final preparations for the launch party, things Dr. Caldwell wanted to handle on her own. Brynn had said she wanted to tag along to see how a big party came together—*how's that for dropping the attitude?*—but really, she wanted to scope out the atrium for any hints of where ACL might hide the bomb.

"I think the investors' dinner went very well," Brynn's

mother was saying. "Although I have to say, the service wasn't great. The waiters kept mixing up orders. And I heard one of them fainted in the hall, caused a commotion—"

"Fainted?" her father echoed. "Was everything okay?"

"Yes, I think so." Dr. Caldwell shifted the car into Park. "Still. It looked unprofessional."

Her mom met Brynn's gaze in the rearview mirror, then looked away. Brynn felt a wave of uneasiness. It wasn't like they'd properly talked after the disastrous dinner. Not a word had been uttered about the accusations Brynn had made; maybe her mother didn't believe them. So what was *that* look for? Was her mother bringing up the fainting caterer because she knew it had been *Brynn*?

That caterer didn't faint, she wanted to shout. *That caterer was threatened. Probably by someone you know.* Someone her mother was in cahoots with, even.

She bit her lip and looked away. Her mother didn't know she'd been there. Brynn was pretty sure she'd convinced her that she wasn't going to blow the whistle. It was still astounding that her mother was this entirely different person. Brynn didn't *want* her mom to be her enemy. She *loved* her mom, and she didn't want to let that love go. But did her mom love her back? If her mom had been involved in giving her Cortexia, it meant she didn't really care about Brynn. All that mattered was Cortexia succeeding. It broke Brynn's heart.

Brynn glanced at her mom in the rearview mirror and

felt daring enough to ask a question. "Was Dr. Lowell at the dinner last night?"

There was a confused wrinkle on her mother's brow. "For a little while, yes. Then he left."

Brynn's father scoffed. "He made you handle everything all by yourself? That doesn't sound like Alfred."

Dr. Caldwell shrugged. "Alfred has been acting a little strangely lately. Not really being a team player." Once again, she gave Brynn a pointed look. Then she kicked the door open and stepped onto the pavement. Brynn felt another wave of uneasiness.

Brynn studied the building ahead of them. BioXin. The huge structure loomed over her, still, strong, and silent, eerie in the midautumn darkness. It terrified her to be here after the attack in the parking lot, but since the launch party was taking place in the atrium, she needed to check out the space, try to figure out what was being planned for the bombing. And anyway, she was with her parents. No one would hurt her with *them* around, right?

They passed through double doors guarded by two guys in dark suits. Brynn's gaze fell to their waists; surely they had guns hidden discreetly under their jackets. Their presence should have made her feel better, but instead, it just increased her sense of unease.

She turned right into the elegant atrium space. It was resplendent, with an indoor garden; a large, burbling fountain; plenty of seating areas; and a ceiling of intricately carved glass. The whole space exuded peacefulness and tranquility, and Brynn understood why her mother would want to have a party here. She could also imagine just how deadly those shards of glass in the ceiling would be if they exploded and came crashing down to the floor.

Dr. Caldwell headed over to the building manager, who waved to her from beside the waterfall. Brynn's father moved in the opposite direction to speak with a few people from the symphony he'd hired to play at the party. Brynn spun around, realizing she was alone. The atrium had a different vibe at night, with no sunlight streaming through the windows. The huge plants everywhere threw off jagged, misshapen shadows, and the waterfalls were so loud they could easily muffle suspicious sounds. She felt a chill wriggle up her spine and sat down on a small bench in the middle of the space. If she stayed visible, no one could corner her and attack her.

Her mother's clogs clunked across the marble floor. The building manager chatted softly about wheelchair accessibility. *Think,* Brynn urged her sluggish brain. If only the soaring space would drum up a memory. Surely she'd been here before, right? Walked around this place with ACL, scoping out where to put the bomb? But what was ACL trying to achieve? Why would they want to blow up scientists and businessmen? Why couldn't they protest more passively? More legally?

She most certainly knew this, once... but there was a dark hole where her memory had been. She surveyed the corners and ceilings. A camera rotated slowly on a post, its steady red beam seeing all. *A camera!* Surveillance video would show people skulking around here, scoping out places to hide a bomb, right? Brynn might see her own image... but she might see who'd worked with her, too. The building manager was only a few feet away; maybe she could figure out a way to ask. But how to do it without tipping off her mom?

The elevator dinged, startling her. Brynn whirled around as the doors opened and a figure stepped out. When Brynn looked into the familiar face, her mouth fell open. Time seemed to stop. There was a moment when both girls just stared at each other as though frozen.

"L-Lexi?" Brynn stammered.

Lexi blinked. Her mouth set into a line. She threw her shoulders back and studied Brynn with renewed confidence. "I hear the launch is Friday," she said evenly, after a long beat.

Brynn stared at her. "Uh, yeah. It is."

Lexi's smile was icy. "Well. I bet it's going to be a great party. Congrats."

She put her head down and hurried past Brynn and out the double doors. Brynn opened her mouth, but no sound came out. Lexi's words seemed to have a double meaning, like they were something Brynn would remember. But there was one problem: She *didn't*.

"Lexi?" Brynn called, starting after her old friend. She stepped onto the pavement and looked right and left. There was a squeal of tires and a cloud of exhaust. A dark blur took a sharp left onto the highway, cutting off oncoming traffic. Brynn blinked, taking in the fast gray shape. It might have been a Corolla. And Lexi might have climbed inside.

"I CAN'T BELIEVE you saw Lexi," Dex said. It was an hour later, after dinner, and they were sitting in Brynn's bedroom. Dex perched on Brynn's desk chair. Brynn was on the bed, massaging her temples. She felt a headache coming on.

"I know," Brynn replied. "I don't understand what she was doing at BioXin."

Dex rubbed his chin. "Do you think *she's* the one texting you, as part of ACL?"

Brynn picked at a loose thread on her jeans. *Could* it be Lexi? She was certainly passionate about standing up for causes. And maybe all those cryptic things she'd said—*I hope you're happy. I bet it's going to be a great party,* even the comment in class about Brynn's bomb report—were actually hints. Did that mean Lexi had been the one to convince Brynn to join ACL, too? How had she coaxed Brynn into building a bomb? Brynn shut her eyes. Lexi had been acting erratic lately, but she couldn't imagine her as a terrorist any more than she could imagine herself as one.

"Maybe you should text her and just ask," Dex suggested.

Brynn gave him a crazy look. "And say what? *Hey, Lexi, are you planning on bombing the Cortexia launch?*"

"Well, we can't go to the cops unless we have some sort of proof," Dex reminded her. "How about you text her, and I'll call the building manager at BioXin. I'll make up something about my mom having her purse stolen in the atrium and wanting to see the security tapes to review what happened. You're right—someone, maybe Lexi, might turn up on a surveillance image. It's worth a shot."

"Okay," Brynn said. She stared at her phone. She had no idea what to say to Lexi. *Hey,* she finally typed. *Can we talk?* She hit the blue Send arrow and waited. The phone made a *swish* noise to indicate the message was now in Lexi's inbox.

Dex studied his phone, too. After a few moments, he pressed it to his ear. Brynn heard the muffled sounds of the line ringing on the other end. "Hello?" Dex said when someone answered. He gave the spiel about his mother's purse and asked if he could see security images. He listened, then said, "Oh?" A moment passed. "Oh." His voice drooped. "Well, all right. Thanks very much, anyway."

Dejected, he hung up and looked at Brynn. "The building

manager says there are no surveillance cameras in the atrium that work at this time."

Brynn blinked at him. "But I saw one. It had a blinking red light, like it had power."

"They just have that light on to fool people. Even the illusion that there's security in a place goes a long way."

"But it's a major drug corporation! Isn't that kind of insane that they don't have proper surveillance?"

"Maybe they don't feel they need it since they have armed guards everywhere," Dex said.

Brynn flopped onto the pillow. Another dead end. "I wish I could just *remember*. I hate relying on other people's memories. All the answers are inside me, but they're in a box I can't open."

"It's scary that Cortexia can be used that way," Dex said. "Something bad happens to someone, and—*bam*—give them some Cortexia, and they'll never know. If it fell into the wrong hands, crimes could be wiped out. Or someone could extract thoughts and beliefs that don't line up with theirs. It's like brainwashing."

Brynn widened her eyes. "I never thought of that. Jesus."

"Right?" Dex chewed on his bottom lip. "But maybe we could figure out a way to get you to remember?"

Brynn looked up. "That would be great. But how?"

He stood up from the chair and walked over to the bed, sitting on the very edge. "Well, you've had other flashes of memory related to when you were thrown into that car. What brought them on?"

Brynn thought for a moment. "Fear," she admitted. "All three times, someone was threatening me, and it brought me back to that time I was interrogated." She closed her eyes, reliving that chilling touch on the back of her neck at the dinner. That whisper in her ear. She looked over at Dex. "Maybe we need to put me in a fearful situation. Then maybe more of it will come back."

Dex shook his head. "No way."

"Why not?"

His expression was tortured. "Brynn. I'm not going to *scare* you."

"But don't you want to know the truth?"

"I do, but . . ." His blue eyes dropped to his lap. "I couldn't do that. I can't see you in pain."

Brynn watched as his hands twitched at his sides. His voice was so fraught with emotion. "Because you don't like seeing anyone in pain . . . or because it's me, specifically?" She knew it was fishing, she knew it made her seem so vulnerable and small, but she couldn't help asking.

Dex's face fell. "Brynn. Because it's *you*."

Brynn's heart did a flip. Slowly, she moved a few inches closer to him so that her leg almost brushed his hip. She didn't dare go any farther, but it seemed like an energy coursed between them, clearly not nothing. Dex didn't pull away.

"When do you think it happened?" Dex asked after a moment. "Being part of ACL, I mean. And when you were thrown into that car."

"The last time I remember clearly was last March. Back then, I was sure Cortexia was this amazing cure. I went on a trip with my mom to Philadelphia to listen to her speak about it at Children's Hospital. I didn't feel like the whole thing was a big lie. So it must have been after that."

"And then what happened?"

"I met Jacob," Brynn admitted. "That was the big thing that changed. He might not be part of this, but things go murky after him. I remember parts of the spring, and then the beginning of the summer. But then, midsummer . . . it's just a blank. Jacob broke up with me. And in that memory when I woke up after being injected, I was lying on my bed, looking out the window. The sun was out. You could tell it was hot. So it was still summer." She pulled her knees to her chest. "I thought I was sad because of Jacob, but I was messed up because of Cortexia, too."

"And when did you start to get your memory back?" Dex asked.

"I started to climb out of it in mid-September." She peeked at him bashfully. "Around the time I met you."

Dex ducked his head. "I remember that first day we spoke." His voice was soft. "The first three weeks, you didn't say a word, but then one day you turned to me and struck up a conversation. You suddenly came alive."

Brynn didn't know what to do with her hands. She'd been so afraid Dex had wiped what had brought the two of them together from his memory. So much had changed, after all. They felt worlds apart now.

"Remember our first date?" she dared to ask. "That freak snow in late September?"

Dex laughed. "We made sleds out of cardboard boxes because no one was selling them yet. We went down the hill at Quiet Waters."

Brynn smiled. "It was so cold, but I didn't care."

"And then we went to that little ice rink. They opened it just for that day."

"You could barely skate." Brynn giggled.

"You had to hold me up." Dex chuckled. "But we got around the rink. You never let me go." He let out a combination of a sniff and a laugh. "I really ..." He trailed off. His cheeks flared red.

"What were you going to say?" Brynn asked softly. "You really ... what?"

When Dex lifted his eyes to hers, his gaze was soft and intimate. Brynn's heart started to pound.

Timidly, she reached forward and lightly touched his hand. Dex didn't pull away. When he looked at her again, the longing in his eyes gave Brynn the courage to shift a little closer. Dex leaned in, too. Brynn held a breath, waiting for his lips to touch hers. But then she heard a huff and pulled away. He was suddenly standing, his hand on the doorknob.

"Brynn, no," he whispered, his voice choked. "I just... can't." And then he hurried out of the room.

EIGHTEEN

Brynn heard the front door open and close. She rushed to the window and watched as Dex jogged to his car and got into the driver's seat. He didn't start the engine. He just sat there.

She forced herself to walk away. The last thing she wanted was for him to look up and see her mooning over him at the window. She didn't need any *more* humiliation right now.

It was over between them. Dex felt for her, maybe, but he didn't love her, *want* her, like he used to. Brynn felt tears come to her eyes. Her mind was still swimming with happy memories of the first date they'd discussed only moments before. Lying next to Dex at the bottom of that sledding hill, watching the flakes fall down on their faces. Holding his hand as they slowly made their way around the ice rink. Sipping from the same cup of hot chocolate, pausing every so often to softly kiss. Brynn understood Dex inside and out, and she was sure he understood her, too. But maybe what he'd discovered about her past was just too much to handle.

She stood and opened her top drawer and pulled out a sports bra, T-shirt, and running shorts. She needed to move her muscles, stop thinking for a while; a night run would be the perfect salve. After she slid on the clothes, she peeked out the window. Dex's car was gone. *Good,* she thought, pushing away the small pang of sadness.

But as she started out the door and down the street, her sneakers making short slaps on the pavement, dread rolled through her again like a thick cloud. Everything, *everything* felt wrong. She still couldn't remember what she'd done and why, but whatever it was, it wouldn't have a good end. Her mother might be caught up in some nefarious government plan. Her father, even. Her grades were a mess. She no longer had a boyfriend. Cortexia was flawed, harming teenage test patients so dramatically the company had sought to cover it up. The news would come out eventually, wouldn't it? And her mother would be shamed and cast out of the research world. Or—an even worse possibility—that bomb would go off at the launch and they'd all be killed. Brynn was never going to figure out who was behind it. If ACL wanted her to know who they were, they would have shown their faces long ago.

She turned into the park, with its rolling hills, small dog run, and ice rink. It was the ice rink, in fact, where she and Dex had spent that magical day in late September. Brynn averted her gaze as she ran past it, knowing that getting even one glimpse would pitch her into even further despair. But as she got to the top of the hill, the ice rink out of view, she suddenly couldn't go another step. She stopped, staring at the trail snaking into the woods. It was so late by now; not a single other person was on the path. The world felt evacuated, suddenly. Empty.

To her left was a small pond that dogs swam in during the summers. Tall weeds surrounded it, waving in the slight breeze. There was something about the pond's murky color, or maybe the moonlight over the water, that reminded Brynn of *Mrs. Dalloway*, which she'd been thinking of quite a bit. Or maybe Virginia Woolf in general. In English class, her teacher had said that Virginia Woolf was so overcome by depression that she'd filled her pockets with stones and walked into a river to drown. Brynn couldn't fathom what sort of anguish the writer must have been going through to do such a thing, but now the act sounded sort of comforting. Dropping into the water inch by inch, first to her knees, then to her waist, then to her shoulders, and then to the top of her head, letting the water fill her lungs and swim through her bloodstream until her heart no longer pumped. *It would be such a release*, Brynn thought. Such a soothing escape.

How long did she stand on the running path, thinking? A few seconds, maybe. Or perhaps minutes. And then, guided by an unseen hand, she found herself at the pond's edge, staring into the inky water. What *was* the point? What was the point to *anything*?

All at once, Brynn didn't want to know what might be worse than jail. Nor did she want to know what was wrong with Cortexia or whether or not her mom was aware of it. She reached out and let the wind kiss her fingertips, trying to get some joy out of the sensation but finding only emptiness. She put one foot into the water, and then the other. It was ice-cold, but after a few seconds of immersion, she became numb. She waded in farther and farther, the water lapping around her hips, then her breasts, then her neck. Her body felt chilled, stilled. The moon was dazzling, but it held no beauty for Brynn, only the sign of another day dead. *Keep walking*, a voice in her head told her. *Only once you're under will you feel better.*

The water was up to her nose now. Brynn took a deep breath, and then it was suddenly like she'd woken from a nightmare. What was she *doing*? She looked around frantically, startled that she couldn't feel her limbs. She took a heavy step under the water, but the ground shifted, and her feet had nothing to hold on to. She tried to scream, but cold water filled her mouth.

"No!" she cried, slipping under the water. Her arms flailed, but they were so numb they felt heavy and useless. She tried to shake off her running shoes, but her ankles were paralyzed. The shore looked miles away from here; how had she waded out so far? "No!" she yelled again, breaking the surface for a gulp of air. Three geese flapped across the moonlit sky. She heard a dog's bark, and then her own desperate splashes. She tried to paddle to the shore, but her arms were stiff, useless. As though caught by a hand at the bottom of the lake, pulling her under, she felt her face slip beneath the surface. Her body began to sink.

Her heart thudded. Her screams poured from her mouth, muffled underwater. The pond snuggled around her like a heavy blanket. Like death. But when she opened her eyes again, she was somewhere else. Strapped to that chair again, with the man in the mask glaring at her. *No.* Brynn fought against the memory. This couldn't be the last thing she saw. She needed something else.

But the memory continued. *Just tell us who you're working with,* the man demanded. *Tell us what you know, and we'll set you free.*

Brynn's eyes darted back and forth. *I—I can't,* she whispered.

He slapped his arms to his sides, coming to attention. Brynn heard footsteps, and she could tell by a shift in the air that someone new was standing over her, though she couldn't see who it was. *Do you really want the terrorists to win?* a new voice growled. *Because that's what's going to happen, you know. And it's going to be* all your fault.

T-They're not terrorists, Brynn whispered. *They just want the truth. We* all *want the truth. Cortexia—*

They *are not entitled to the truth,* this new voice interrupted. Brynn knew the voice. But why? *It's up to you now. You hold the key. You can change their minds.*

But I don't want *to change their minds!* Brynn bleated.

So that means you want our country to continue to be rocked by terror? Do you really want to be responsible for that?

The first man snickered. *I told you we should have taken care of this a long time ago.*

The second voice sighed with resignation. When he spoke again, his voice was farther away, as if he'd stepped to the other side of the room. *Fine. Do it.*

Out came the zippered pouch. BIOXIN, read the logo on the front. *No!* Brynn called. *You can't do this to me! This isn't right!*

The man in the surgical mask just stared. *Don't worry. Soon enough, it won't matter. You won't remember.*

A scream froze in Brynn's throat. *Just stop,* said the second voice. And just like that, Brynn realized why she recognized it. It was so *obvious,* suddenly. So clean and clear.

But just as she had that epiphany, the lights snapped off, and the memory faded. She didn't feel cold anymore. She felt . . . *nothing.* When a tiny bead of light shone before her eyes, she thought it was some sort of trick. But then the bead expanded into a small, marble-sized circle. It radiated outward, growing larger and larger, until her whole field of vision was filled with so much brightness that she had to squint. A haloed shadow blotted the light. As Brynn's vision adjusted, she saw a familiar face. But it didn't make sense. What was he doing here?

"D-Dex?" she stammered.

All at once, consciousness snapped back. She felt frigid air on her wet, bare skin. Dex stared down at her, tears in his eyes. "Brynn," he was moaning. "Oh, God. *Brynn.*"

Brynn tried to lift her tongue in her mouth, but it felt weighted down. Seemingly a million feet away were her bare feet, poking out over the grass. She dared to wiggle a toe. Then a finger. She looked at Dex again. "W-What happened?"

Dex's smile was fragile. He took her hand. "I saw you go into the park, and I almost didn't get to you before—" He broke off to swallow a sob. "Brynn, you almost *drowned.* What were you thinking? Why were you in that pond?"

Brynn stared at him. *Because my boyfriend didn't want to kiss me* didn't seem like a good excuse. But why *had* she gone in? Temporary insanity?

It was baffling. Walking into that pond, feeling like it was the only answer—it was like a monster had taken control of her body, forcing her at gunpoint. She'd never done something like that before . . . *had* she? Her memory was so murky. She was reminded again of what Lexi said about her at the restaurant, that she could be volatile. Were there elements of Brynn's personality that she'd blocked out since receiving Cortexia? Or had the drug changed her in a violent, shocking way?

Brynn felt tears come to her eyes. "I don't know. It was like something came over me." And then she told him about the latest flashback she'd had. She took a deep breath, the man's face and voice coalescing in her thoughts. "Senator Merriweather was there," she whispered, almost afraid to say it too loudly. "In that room, injecting me with Cortexia."

Dex's eyes widened. "Are you *sure*?"

She nodded, the memory snapping back. She heard him say, *Soon enough, it won't matter. You won't remember.* He was doing exactly what Dex feared: using the drug to brainwash her and wipe out a dangerous memory. "It was definitely him. He's in on it."

"What do you remember?"

She kept her eyes shut, desperate to remember everything. "He kept saying something about *the terrorists*. Like how if I didn't help him, the terrorists were going to win. I thought he meant the people in ACL were terrorists, and I insisted they *weren't*—they just wanted the truth. But now I'm not sure he was talking about the people in ACL. Maybe he meant someone else."

"So he meant *real* terrorists?"

"I think so." A strange feeling was beginning to fill her. "Remember what you said about how Cortexia could be used to brainwash people? What if that's the reason BioXin is so hell-bent on getting Cortexia out into the world? Maybe there's a government contract for it or something. Maybe we're going to round up terrorists, then inject them with my mom's serum, then forcefully wipe out their ideologies."

Dex's mouth twisted incredulously. "That sounds crazy."

But Brynn wasn't so sure. "Have you heard Merriweather on TV? This is exactly what he's always talking about. The scary thing is that it's a slippery slope. One day you're drugging someone who's a real threat, but the next it could just be someone who's pro-choice instead of pro-life, or vice versa. What if Merriweather decided to run for president? Would he round up the whole country and give them all Cortexia so they'd forget anything he ever did wrong? It would be like a dictatorship. And no one would even *know* what he was doing because he'd have the power to change memories and thoughts."

"God," Dex whispered. "Maybe you're right."

Brynn felt pretty convinced, too. "And maybe ACL got wind of their grand plan. No wonder they're wary and want the medication off the shelves. They have to do something before Merriweather erases the memories of anyone who can stop him."

"But do you really think that deserves a *bomb*?" Dex whispered.

"No. Of course not. But if we figure out who's in ACL and explain who they're up against—the military, the people who injected me—maybe we can get closer to working this out peacefully." She licked her lips, realizing that maybe she and Dex were now in a different place than they were earlier today. "I mean, if you still want to work with me. I understand if you want to bail. This is all so complicated."

Dex sank down next to her, keeping watch on the trail. "It *is* complicated. And yeah, I'd rather be hanging out with friends right now. Running. Doing something simple. Being seventeen years old."

Brynn pulled her knees to her chest. *Well, there you go.*

"I'm just . . . scared." Dex ran his hand down his face. "So much of the way you were acting reminded me of the way Marc was when he came back. You remind me of him anyway—your spark, your determination, how easily I can talk to you. But when you became paranoid, secretive, when you couldn't remember things—well, it brought back a lot of haunting memories about my brother. I know the situations are totally different, but it still struck a chord . . . and I had to step back. I had to push you away." Dex looked ashamed. "I was so afraid of losing you like I lost him. So I thought it would be easier just not to care."

Brynn let out a breath she hadn't realized she was holding. Everything Dex had just said was such a relief that the anger she'd felt toward him instantly dissolved. "It makes

NINETEEN

TWO DAYS TO LAUNCH

When Brynn awoke on Wednesday morning, she was in her own bed, kissed by cool, fresh sheets and a soft down pillow. Winter sun streamed through her window, and her little bedside fan, which she couldn't sleep without, whirred soothingly. There was a solid, comforting warmth beside her, and she curled into it, sleepily smacking her lips. Dex's hair was mussed, and his eyelashes were matted adorably with sleep. "Mmm," Brynn said, wrapping her arm around his bare chest and hugging him closer. Dex murmured with pleasure.

There was a call from downstairs. "Brynn? You up?"

Brynn's eyes shot open. It was morning. She had school soon. And *Dex* was in her bed. The previous night flashed sense." She tilted her head so that it touched his shoulder. "I'm sorry I reminded you of him."

"Don't be sorry. Maybe it was good for me to face my past. But it doesn't mean I have to continue to push you away. If that's okay with you . . ."

Brynn looked up, wanting to make sure she was reading what he'd said correctly. Dex took the sides of her face in his hands. Something warm and excited rushed through Brynn's body, bringing tingles to her lips.

"That's okay with me," she breathed.

Dex leaned forward and kissed her lips. The kiss felt gentle and sweet, and she closed her eyes, trying to drink it in. It was so *right* to kiss Dex. No one else mattered in the world. But as hard as she tried to focus on the kiss and only the kiss, the same grisly interrogation scene popped into her mind again. And she kept seeing Senator Merriweather's face so close, his mouth twisted, his eyes wild. She kept seeing him pull the trigger to give her that shot of Cortexia, punctuating his decision with a derisive, all-powerful laugh.

back to her. Dex had walked her home after they'd talked about Senator Merriweather being part of the Cortexia brainwashing plot. They hadn't wanted to continue the conversation on Brynn's doorstep, so she'd invited Dex inside, sneaking him upstairs and into her bedroom, where he waited while she rinsed off her experience in the pond. She'd intended to keep talking to Dex afterward, but instead, they'd fallen onto the bed and started kissing.

And then, after many hours, they'd fallen asleep.

Then a knock sounded. "Brynn." Her mother's voice was sharp. "Are you in there?"

Brynn poked Dex in the back. *"Wake up,"* she whispered.

Dex opened one eye, then the other, then stretched his arms over his head. But he was going too slowly, so Brynn grabbed him by both hands to stand. Dex was about to groan, but Brynn covered his mouth with her palm.

"In here," she said, shoving him into her closet. Stumbling, Dex groggily fell face-first among a pile of Brynn's old T-shirts. She shut the closet door as best she could, then looked down at herself. At least she had on a T-shirt and pajama pants. She checked in the mirror on the back of the door and was satisfied that she didn't have any hickeys on her neck and that her lips weren't bruised from kissing. Rolling back her shoulders, she whipped the door open and smiled brightly at her mom. "Good morning."

But then she remembered everything. The smile melted from her face. *Senator Merriweather.* He and Brynn's mom had been talking so gaily at that investors' dinner. The man who'd kidnapped her own daughter and forced Cortexia on her.

"Brynn." Her mother sounded flustered, but then she looked at Brynn more closely and cocked her head. "What?"

Brynn's mouth felt dry. *I know what you did,* she wanted to say. *And I know who you're working with.* She was dying to say it. It was so tempting.

Then, suddenly, Dr. Caldwell's phone rang. The noise startled both of them. Brynn's mom glanced at the screen, then back to Brynn. "I need to take this." She seemed reluctant as she put the phone to her ear, but she still edged out of the room, then was gone.

Brynn shut the door and collapsed against it. She felt drained. Then she remembered the closet. She crept over to it and knocked softly. "Hurry up," she called to Dex. "She's gone."

Dex slunk out with an impish grin. "That was quite a wake-up call."

She tossed Dex his pants. "Here. We have to get you out of here before anyone sees you."

"Okay, okay." Dex flopped onto the bed. "What's next in our plan? Go to the police? Tell them the news about Merriweather?" Dex shoved one foot into a sneaker. "If the government is condoning brainwashing, the world needs to know about it."

"We can't tell the press yet." Brynn pulled open the

window to usher Dex out of the house. "We don't have anything on Merriweather besides my memory. I wish we still had that BioXin file, because at least that would stall Cortexia's production. But I'm sure that's been destroyed by now—probably by BioXin. They all must be working together, against ACL. Which is exactly why ACL wants to bomb the launch."

"And still nothing from Lexi?" Dex asked as he climbed onto the roof.

Brynn's gaze fell to her phone. "Nothing." She sent another text to Lexi, not feeling very hopeful her old friend would reply. Then, while Dex sat on the windowsill, she picked up her phone and dialed the main number to the lab. Because it was regular office hours, a receptionist answered.

"Dr. Alfred Lowell, please," Brynn said briskly. There was a pause, and the phone rang again. Brynn jiggled her toe impatiently. After four rings, the call went to voice mail. *"Hello, you have reached Dr. Alfred Lowell at Halcyon. I will be on vacation from November fourteenth to November seventeenth. If you have any questions, please contact Dr. Celeste Caldwell, at..."*

"Vacation?" Brynn squeaked, pulling the receiver away from her ear while Lowell's voice droned on. "The launch is in two days! Why would he go on a trip *now*?"

Dex's expression was dark. "Unless he was sent away."

Brynn felt a chill. "Do you think?" She thought of her mom's words after the investors' dinner: *Alfred has been acting a little strangely lately. Not really being a team player.* What if he'd expressed his concerns about Cortexia and they'd forced him out?

The beep for Lowell's voice mail startled her. She peered at Dex, still half out the window. *"Should I leave a message?"* she whispered, covering her phone's microphone with her thumb.

Dex shook his head. "We can't have our voices in that guy's inbox. As far as you know, your mom thinks you haven't caught on yet, but that doesn't mean Merriweather isn't listening in to everything happening at BioXin. We have to keep a low profile until we figure this all out."

He was right. Brynn hit End. "Fine. If Lowell isn't going to talk, we need to find out what's going on for ourselves."

Dex's mouth twisted. "Meaning?"

Brynn thought it over, then looked at Dex with determination. "Nail Merriweather. Get him good."

Dex nodded. "If we can expose Merriweather and his plan, then the launch will be canceled. Meaning no bomb." He leaned forward and kissed her, then shimmied down the roof. For the first time in days, Brynn felt secure again. She and Dex were back together. A team.

She hoped they'd never part again.

TWENTY

THE DAY BEFORE THE LAUNCH

"This is ridiculous," Brynn said, shifting her weight in the passenger seat of Dex's car. "Maybe we have the wrong information?"

Dex looked at his phone again. "According to C-SPAN, Merriweather just finished giving a speech to Congress about war contracts in Iraq. He's going to appear on those stairs any minute."

It was four P.M. on Thursday, the day before Cortexia's launch. Brynn and Dex sat in Dex's Jeep on a side street that bordered the U.S. Capitol. They'd been watching the steps for a half hour already, and while plenty of other high-powered political figures had descended in the last hour—the majority whip, a famous Congressman who'd had an affair scandal a few years ago, and even the vice president—Senator Merriweather seemed to have dissolved into thin air.

Brynn perused her phone again. Some liberal websites had plenty of nasty things to say about Senator Merriweather, but she wasn't sure if any of it was useful in connecting him to the Cortexia plot. For example: Despite all of his praise for the sciences and his encouragement that more women apply for STEM-based jobs, Merriweather had made a lot of pro-racial-profiling comments on a conservative website. It appeared he wasn't as decorated in battle as he'd claimed, either, having stretched the truth about some of his tours of duty. One commenter said that Merriweather had a secret family in Canada through whom he funneled secret funds to Russian terrorists, but Brynn couldn't find any evidence of that. And there was nothing about Cortexia. Nothing about PTSD. Nothing about BioXin.

She typed *Senator Merriweather* and *BioXin* into the search engine next. A few stories from the *New York Times* and *Slate* appeared, recapping the investors' dinner from a few nights before, but it wasn't odd that Merriweather had attended—military matters and soldier welfare were some of his prime platforms. There were several photos of him and a few marines who'd attended the dinner. Merriweather's smile seemed warm enough, but his eyes were cold and calculating. Brynn knew that how Cortexia had saved those soldiers didn't matter to him. It just served as a cover.

Dex sat up straighter and pointed. *"There!"*

Brynn craned her neck. Merriweather, dressed in a sharp suit and carrying an expensive-looking leather brief-case, bounded down the stairs of the Capitol. He was deep in conversation with two younger guys, maybe aides. All three men ducked into a black car waiting at the curb, and the car pulled away.

"Let's follow him," Brynn whispered.

Dex nodded and gunned the engine. The traffic was moving at a crawl, but they were able to fall into the same lane as the senator's vehicle, and just two cars behind. They weaved through the city, ending up on the road that bordered the Potomac River.

"Where do you think we're going?" Brynn murmured, noting that Dex's knuckles were white as he gripped the steering wheel. "Virginia?" According to her research, the senator lived in Virginia. It would be a disappointment if the car was just taking him home.

"Not sure," Dex said.

Suddenly the senator's car veered away from the river toward American University. Dex wove through the streets, desperate to keep sight of the government license plate. Twice, the senator's car seemed to slow, its occupants perhaps sensing they were being followed.

"Let some cars get between us and them," Brynn whispered, and Dex obliged. The senator's car continued on.

Finally, the car stopped at an office building on the edge

of the campus. There weren't any lights on, the patch of grass by the front door was shabby and full of weeds, and a stack of takeout menus was wedged under the front door. Dex parked in a concealed lot across the street that gave them an unobstructed view. The senator and his cohorts exited the vehicle and walked toward the building's entrance. One of his aides glanced around cautiously, then moved on.

Only when they disappeared through the front door did Brynn let out a breath. "What do you think they're doing in there? Does it have something to do with Cortexia?"

"No idea." Dex looked around. "Does this place seem familiar to you? Maybe this is where they brought you when you were interrogated?"

Brynn inspected the small bench by the entrance, the derelict-looking Sunoco station across the street, and a small, sad bus stop that bore a billboard ad for some sort of low-cost car insurance. "I had a bag over my head. It could have been anywhere."

Dex typed the building's address into his phone, only to find that the building had once housed an orthodontist's office and a few other random companies whose names told them nothing. Brynn studied the building's mostly empty parking lot again and noticed a vehicle she hadn't seen before. Her blood turned to ice.

"Look." She gestured, and Dex stared out the window. Slowly, the recognition registered on his face.

"The gray Corolla," he whispered.

Brynn's heart pounded. Even without a view of the license plate, she knew this was the same car that had stalked her. So the car didn't belong to someone from ACL at all. It made sense. Of *course* Merriweather's people had followed her around; they needed to keep her in check and make sure she didn't remember anything before the launch. Her heart began to pound. It had been good for her and Dex to follow the senator today. Whatever was happening inside had to do with Cortexia.

"We need to call the police," she whispered. "Let's think of a reason for them to come."

Dex twisted his mouth. "We could stage a robbery?"

"Call in a bomb threat?" Brynn suggested, then clamped her mouth shut. She didn't want to be associated with any bombs whatsoever, even imaginary ones.

Then she remembered her license plate search. "The Corolla's plate isn't registered. Maybe we could say we're pretty sure it's stolen, like we saw something suspicious happen when the person pulled in here, and we want the cops to check it out?"

But then she saw the flaws. "Then again, if the police show up and they can't bust Merriweather on anything, he'll know we're spying on him. He'll shut down the operation. I'll get injected again."

Leaning across the car, she grabbed the keys out of the ignition. "We have to move on to plan B and go in there."

Dex looked uncertain. "Are you serious?"

"Yeah." She tucked the keys into her pocket. "We need to get video evidence. Take pictures. Get something we can turn over to the cops."

"But..." Dex's eyes darted back and forth. "What if they catch us? Then they'll inject you for sure. *And* me!"

Brynn shrugged. "I have to take this chance. I can go in myself if you want...."

Dex looked at her like she was crazy. He unbuckled his seat belt. "I'm not letting you go in there alone." As he swung out of the car, he gave her an approving look over the hood. "You're something, you know that? I like this new Brynn."

Brynn cocked her head. "What do you mean?"

"You're so brave. So determined. It's hot."

Brynn rolled her eyes. "Don't make me into a sex symbol, Kinsley." Still, she begrudgingly accepted a kiss from him on the cheek.

From the trunk, they took out wigs, dark glasses, and hoodies; they couldn't risk being recognized. After putting everything on, they waited for a break in traffic and crossed the street. When they passed the gray Toyota, Brynn couldn't resist peeking in. The car was empty. The carpeted seat backs looked freshly vacuumed. The middle console didn't have a speck of dirt. Coins were neatly lined up in their appropriate slots. It was like the car had just been driven off the lot. Generic. Indistinguishable. She peered at the license plate again, wondering if there was a different one beneath it; the group could peel this plate off, reveal the real one, and no one could connect this car to anything sinister.

Their footsteps rang out as they crossed the parking lot. As Dex opened the front door, Brynn winced at the garish *screech*. Inside was a dingy hallway lined in graying tile. She couldn't hear anything coming from behind any of the doors; did anyone work in this place? She tiptoed to the first door and peered through its windowed top half. Inside was a large, blank room. No desks. No furnishings. No waiting area.

A hollow *thud* sounded above their heads, and they froze. Brynn pointed at a door marked STAIRS. Dex nodded, and they went through and started climbing. Brynn's stomach quivered with nerves as they ascended.

The second floor was laid out just like the first, a simple hallway with several offices on both sides. There were faded spots on the walls where pictures had once hung, and an ancient, crushed Coke can lay upended on the floor. A fluorescent bulb flickered over their heads, and it seemed chillier up here, as though they'd climbed into a refrigerator. Another *clunk* sounded from behind an office door marked in faded letters reading LRD INC. Brynn's skin prickled. She heard murmurs—a male voice, and then a deeper male voice. Was one of them Merriweather?

She tiptoed toward the door. There were more murmurs. Someone coughed. What if Merriweather opened the door and saw them? What if they had guards stationed throughout the building?

She crouched down just outside the door and pressed her ear to the wall. The murmurs began to escalate. It was turning into an argument. Another voice began to speak, and Brynn swore she heard the words *Up the ante.* She exchanged a worried look with Dex. *Up the ante?* What did that mean?

Dex's phone rang.

It was such a silly little noise—a dreamy scale on a xylophone. Brynn had gone through his ringtones with him one day when they were bored, choosing specific tones for her, his mom, and his dad. The ring reverberated off the walls, seemingly gaining volume with each note. Dex stared at the phone for a horrified beat, then fumbled for it to shut it up. The silence afterward was deafening. Slowly, Dex glanced toward the closed door. *Please, please let them not have heard that,* Brynn willed. *Please keep on talking.*

The door flew open so forcefully it crashed against the wall, creating a loud boom. Brynn spun around and darted into the first office to her right, thankfully finding it unlocked. She pulled the door shut behind her and crouched in the shadows, her heart banging in her chest. Footsteps rang out in the hall. Were the men going after Dex? Brynn heard shouts, then a slam. Tears came to her eyes. She should have listened to Dex. They should never have come here.

Silence followed. The office was dark and empty, with a large, square window that faced the parking lot. Her nose twitched from the carpet dust. Brynn was desperate to peek outside, so she crept to the window, slipped off her sunglasses, and peeked out.

Something flashed out of the corner of her eye. Out the window, a figure in a dark wig and sunglasses sprinted across the parking lot. *Dex.* Brynn leaned in to get a closer look. Dex looked over his shoulder, then dove into the bushes. Moments later, a man chased through the lot after him. It wasn't Merriweather, nor one of the aides she'd seen with him on the Capitol steps, but as he turned around, Brynn instantly knew she'd met him before. He might have had a surgical mask on the last time, but she'd have known those squinty, forbidding eyes anywhere. It was the first man from her memory. The guy who'd interrogated her.

You have to get a picture of him. Trembling, Brynn reached for her phone, but it was wedged far into her pocket, and she was too nervous about what was going to happen to Dex. She watched helplessly as the man hunted for him, but Dex seemed well hidden in the bushes. Finally, the man slapped his hands to his sides and stormed back to the building. Brynn looked over her shoulder, worried he might come for her next. She needed to get out of here.

A small shuffling noise sounded from a back room. Brynn froze. There was more shuffling, then what sounded like a sigh. She squinted into the dusty darkness. There was a door to her right. Another noise sounded, reminding her of a whimper. Was someone hurt?

Brynn dared to take a step toward the door. The floorboard creaked, and she winced. Then she heard a desperate "Mmf!" Her eyes widened. It, too, was coming from that back room.

"Mmf!"

Her heart strained against her ribs as she took another step toward the door and slowly pulled it open. The dark room beyond, its window shaded, smelled like sweat. Something bulky twisted in the corner—a person. Brynn could just make out a head, and maybe a hand. Whoever it was seemed *tied* to something, unable to move. Then the figure froze, alert.

Brynn reached for her phone, clicked on the flashlight function, and pointed it toward the figure in the corner. There was another desperate, fearful *mmf*. The beam of light traveled over bound wrists, shackled ankles. A torso wriggled futilely to get free. Mustering up her courage, Brynn aimed the beam of light at the person's face. She was so startled that the phone almost slipped from her fingers. Her mouth dropped open, and for a few moments, she couldn't say a word.

It was *Lexi*.

TWENTY-ONE

Brynn started to undo the binding on Lexi's wrists. "Oh my God, oh my God," she whispered, her hands trembling as she pulled the heavy tape from Lexi's mouth. There were sticky marks on Lexi's cheeks where the duct tape had been. Her eyes were puffy from crying. She smelled like she might have lost control of her bladder. Her hair was matted around her head, and her eyes darted nervously back and forth. Her friend let out a breath when the tape was off, then looked at Brynn with confusion. Brynn pulled off her wig. Lexi's brow furrowed.

"You?" Lexi cried. "Why are *you* here?"

"I'm wondering the same thing," Brynn said in astonishment.

Lexi wiped her eyes. Her hands were trembling. "S-Someone grabbed me from behind. Put a bag over my head, knocked me out. Where *are* we? What's going on?"

It made no sense, but there was no time for questions now. Brynn glanced over her shoulder, trying to figure out how to get them both out of here immediately. A small window on the other side of the room led to a roof overhang, much like the roof outside her house. If they could crawl out the window to the overhang, maybe they'd be able to drop down without really hurting themselves.

"Come on," she whispered, stuffing the wig back on her head and helping Lexi to her feet. They hurried across the room to the window and pushed it open. Brynn searched the parking lot; the coast was clear. She shoved Lexi out the window first, then crawled out after her. Outside, the sky above was gray and flat. There wasn't a soul in the parking lot or on the street; this was their chance. Brynn scrambled down the face of the roof and dropped to the ground, signaling for Lexi to follow. Lexi balked, but then did as she was told. As her feet hit the pavement, she let out a pained wail.

"*Shh!*" Brynn hissed, terrified someone might hear them.

"*Sorry,*" Lexi snapped as she hobbled across the pavement. She glanced back at the building. "Who did this to me? Do you know?"

"Maybe," Brynn said, realizing Lexi had no clue what

she'd just stepped into. But how was that possible? Why was Lexi *here*?

She grabbed Lexi's hand and dragged her into the same bushes Dex had cut through. But he wasn't there anymore. His absence worried her—where had he gone? What if someone had captured him? She glanced at her phone, but she was too afraid to send him a text quite yet. She didn't want his phone to give him away like it had just a few minutes earlier. *Please be okay, Dex,* she willed silently. *Run fast. Just get out of here.*

They waited for a few minutes, watching the building. Its windows were so dirty, it was difficult to tell what was going on inside. But soon enough, the group was going to notice Lexi was gone, right? They needed to get as far away from here as possible.

"Come on." She pulled Lexi out of the bushes and across the street. As they cut through the lot where they'd parked, Brynn noticed that Dex's Jeep was gone. She let out a sigh of relief. He must have been able to drive away, which meant he was more than likely safe. But what about them? How would *they* get out of here?

She turned onto a thoroughfare toward the center of campus and was relieved to see people ahead.

"Brynn, what's going on?" Lexi cried. "Where are we going? Why aren't you telling me?"

"Shhh," Brynn murmured. "We can't talk about anything until I find somewhere that's safe." Up ahead, she noticed a bunch of fitness machines in a window. Beefy guys were lifting weights in the back of the room. Merriweather and his goons wouldn't think to look for them in a gym, would they? And even if they did come in, guns blazing, there were more than enough people to serve as witnesses and to call the police. It didn't hurt that some of them were strong, bulky weightlifters.

She pulled Lexi into the gym, practically tossing some cash at the girl at the front desk for the daily fee and scribbling down fake names and addresses on the guest pass form they were required to fill out. Then she bought two ball caps from the accessories shop.

Lexi stared at her like she had two heads. "What are we doing?"

"We'll be safe in here," Brynn explained.

"Safe from *what*?"

Brynn wasn't sure what to tell her. Maybe her logic was crazy, but she figured if she let enough time pass, Merriweather's goons wouldn't be looking for them anymore. Hopefully, the goons didn't get an ID on *her* at all.

She tossed Lexi one of the caps. "Put this on." Then she pointed at a nearby treadmill that faced the opposite wall, away from the windows. "Start walking on that. And we'll talk."

Lexi blinked at the machine. "But I'm *exhausted*." Brynn gave her a sharp look, and Lexi slouched onto the treadmill and pressed Start. Brynn chose the one next to her and started walking.

"Those guys who tied you up and threw you in that room," Brynn murmured as the belt started to move. "Are you sure you don't know them? Are you sure you don't know what they wanted?"

Lexi shook her head. "I didn't even really *see* them. But no. I—I have no idea. Money from my parents? Was it a kidnapping?"

Brynn considered that for a moment, then ruled it out. There was really only one conclusion that made any sense; it annoyed her that Lexi wouldn't just come out and say it. "You know, for someone mysteriously texting me for the past week, telling me I'm one of you, you definitely aren't making this very easy."

Lexi stared at her. "Huh?"

"Come on, Lexi. Drop the act. I know what's been going on, okay? You've been trying to jog my memory that there's something wrong with Cortexia. You succeeded, because now I remember. Well, sort of."

Lexi stopped, and the belt shot her backward. She had to hold on to the machine's handles to keep from falling off. "Cortexia is just about the last thing I thought we'd talk about today."

Brynn frowned. "Why not?"

Lexi snorted. "What do you mean? You know why not."

Now Brynn felt totally confused. "Actually, I don't. I'm having memory issues. It's a long story, but I think I was injected with Cortexia to wipe out some stuff I discovered. So I need you to fill me in on what you know and what's going on."

Lexi's eyes widened. "You were injected with Cortexia? *Shit.*" For a moment, the only sounds were the *pound-pound-pound* of Lexi's feet. "You really don't remember us talking about this?"

"No." Brynn felt excited . . . and desperate. Maybe, finally, she was going to get some solid answers. "I need you to tell me again. *Please.*"

Lexi pressed her lips together. She stared blankly at the wall, a look of regret on her face. "Okay. Well, first of all, I was in a clinical trial last year."

Brynn felt a jolt. Yet another surprise. "*You?* Why?"

"Because of the robbery. My psychologist said I had PTSD. I thought it would help. I wasn't sleeping. I kept having visions of what happened. I just needed it to stop."

There was a ringing sound in Brynn's ears. "Wh-Who ran the trial?"

Lexi stared at her feet as they trudged on the machine. "Your mom. *Duh.* You don't remember that, either?"

Brynn shook her head, but she wasn't surprised. Her mother had pretty much admitted her guilt, after all.

"I think I got the placebo," Lexi went on. "I was disappointed at first, but then, after everything that I found out, maybe it was a good thing I didn't get the real drug."

"After you found out *what*?"

Lexi looked uncomfortable. She adjusted the brim on her cap. "I got to know some of the other kids in the trial. We kept in touch. But one by one, each of them seemed to vanish. I had a weird feeling about them. So I started calling their families. Turns out three kids I'd been in the trial with died—suicide in each case." She let out a mirthless laugh. *"Three kids."*

A chill whipped through Brynn's body. She gripped the handles on the sides of the treadmill. "You think it was because of Cortexia?"

Lexi rolled her eyes. "You don't believe me, do you? You didn't the first time I told you, either. But yes, I'm pretty sure it was because of Cortexia. Everyone in the trial was a hot mess, but none of us were suicidal. And then, voilà. Some people got injected with the real deal, and all of a sudden they pulled the trigger, pun intended."

Brynn's head spun. Were these the negative results in teens that BioXin was trying to cover up? Instead of curing patients, the drug worked differently on teenage brains, making them *worse*. It was backfiring—kind of like an anti-SSRI, triggering suicide instead of preventing it.

Suddenly it felt so obvious. Was this why she'd had the mysterious but driving desire to plunge into the water last night, maybe ending her life? Was her Cortexia injection ravaging her still-growing and changing brain, pushing her to make decisions she normally wouldn't dream of?

She faced Lexi. "I got mad at you when you told me the first time?" she asked slowly. "Was that what caused our fight on my front porch?"

"I shouldn't have kept from you that I was in the trial, especially because it was your mom's drug. But your mom swore everyone in the trial to secrecy. We had to sign an agreement. And afterward, when I came to you, you wouldn't even *listen*, Brynn. You acted like I'd made it up."

The argument began to shimmer into view in Brynn's mind. Lexi told her about her three friends from the trial who'd died. And then Brynn had gotten angry—*really* angry.

How do you know they didn't get placebos, too? Brynn had argued. Lexi just shrugged. *Because I'm still fine. I don't want to kill myself.* She'd tried to sidestep Brynn. *Let me in. Your mom needs to know what's going on.*

Brynn caught her arm. *I'm not going to let you ruin this for her. My mother sacrificed so much to get where she is today. She worked hard in the lab, skipping weekends and holidays and birthdays just so she could get this right. She's a good person. If people are killing themselves, it has to be because of another reason.*

Lexi stared at Brynn with a mix of shock and sadness. *I don't see it that way. And I think everyone should know the truth.*

I can't let you do that, Brynn challenged her. *I can't let you tell my mom.*

Lexi crossed her arms over her chest. *You're not thinking straight.*

Now Brynn turned to her friend, suddenly certain. "You told someone else, didn't you? And you guys organized, became the Anti-Cortexia League." She pointed at Lexi. "And I came around to see your point of view, didn't I? I worked with you—but I was given Cortexia to block out the memory. Which is why you've been texting me."

Lexi's blue eyes narrowed. "I haven't been texting you. And I have no idea what the Anti-Cortexia League is."

"Come on. That's why I saw you at BioXin the other day, right? You were scoping it out for the launch. And that's why you kept making those veiled comments about how *happy* you were for me and how great a party the launch was going to be—you were trying to jog my memory. You were trying to tell me that *you* are part of what's happening. You can *tell* me. It's okay. I'm not going to turn you in."

A long beat passed. A light flashed on Lexi's treadmill, indicating she'd walked a quarter mile. "Brynn . . . ," she said in a small, weak, scared voice. "Look, I didn't tell anyone else about Cortexia's side effects besides you. I wasn't crazy about the decision, but I also didn't want to destroy your family. I was at BioXin the other day because my clinical trial was paid, and I was there to collect my hundred bucks. It took forever for the checks to come in. I guess BioXin saved some money, being that some of the trial volunteers they were supposed to pay are now dead." Then she gave Brynn a strange look. "But wait. Are you saying *you're* in a protest group against your mom's drug? What are you planning on doing at the launch?"

Brynn's throat felt dry. She wanted to tell Lexi about the bomb, but suddenly she felt ashamed. Was Lexi telling the truth? Did she really know *nothing*?

When Brynn didn't answer, Lexi continued, "As for those comments about the launch, yeah, I was still bitter about our fight. I still don't think Cortexia should be released to the public." Lexi's voice was steady, unwavering. Brynn saw no telltale signs that she was lying. "I thought you still didn't believe me. And yes, that's why we aren't friends anymore, at least from my perspective. This isn't some weird mind game I'm playing with you, Brynn. I definitely haven't sent you texts."

"So who did?" Brynn asked, more to herself than to Lexi.

Lexi was quiet for a moment. The treadmill belt hummed noisily. "I don't know. When did you join this group? Do you remember?"

"This summer, I think. Or maybe the spring."

"So you were dating Jacob then." Lexi's expression was suddenly closed off. "Maybe he has something to do with it."

Brynn lowered her eyes. "I thought so, too, but now I'm not sure." She breathed out. "I'm just . . . *stunned*. I don't understand why you were tied up if you aren't part of ACL. You don't pose a threat. Why would they hurt you?"

"Who are *they*?" Lexi demanded.

Brynn looked right and left, then figured it was probably safe to tell her. She explained as simply as she could. When she mentioned Merriweather's name, Lexi looked sick. "*That* guy," she whispered. "It totally makes sense. He's pure evil."

"But what would he want with you?"

Lexi's throat bobbed. "Maybe because I was part of the clinical trial. Maybe just knowing what happened is dangerous."

Brynn looked at her. Could that be true? What if Merriweather and his cohorts were worried about every kid who'd been part of the clinical trial, and they planned to inject each and every one of them so they'd forget? That might be one of the reasons they needed that folder back from Brynn—so they could figure out who the test patients were and systematically kidnap them.

Lexi hit the Stop button on the treadmill and stood on the machine, staring at Brynn. "Do you think those people are going to come after me again?"

"I don't know." Brynn hit her own Stop button. "But you have to be careful." She shut her eyes, feeling a pang of guilt. "I'm sorry you got mixed up in this," she said softly. "And I should have listened to you when you told me about Cortexia the first time."

Brynn opened her eyes to see Lexi's face was still stony. "I've missed you a lot. Ever since last spring, you've pretended like I don't exist."

"You haven't treated me that great, either," Brynn protested, but then she felt petty; the last thing she wanted to do was get into another argument. And anyway, maybe it *was* her fault. Jacob had pushed her away from everything she loved. "But why did you ask me that question about bombs while I was doing my report the other day?" she asked.

A wrinkle formed on Lexi's brow, and she lowered her eyes. "When we argued about Cortexia, you were like, *What are you going to do, Lexi? Bomb my mom's lab?*"

"I *said* that?"

"Yeah. But I knew you didn't mean it. And I deserved it. I came to you with guns blazing, blaming your mom. It wasn't fair."

A man at the back of the room dropped a set of free weights with a clang, and Brynn jumped. But no one was coming for them. No one here knew who they were. She took a deep breath. "Is this why you told Dex I was volatile? Because I didn't believe you?"

Lexi cocked her head. "Wait, what?"

"When Dex went over to talk to you at Growler's, you told him I was volatile and unpredictable. But I was never like that, except maybe in that last argument. Was I?"

Lexi's eyes narrowed. For a moment, something Brynn

couldn't decipher flashed across her eyes. A long beat passed, and another set of free weights crashed to the ground. Lexi took a breath. "Brynn, I don't—"

A blur passed outside the gym, stealing Brynn's attention. She froze, terrified it might be someone from Merriweather's crew. The figure stopped, then pushed through the door. Brynn grabbed Lexi's hand, but as the figure stepped into the light, she saw Dex's close-cropped hair and green army jacket.

"Oh my God." He spied her on the treadmill and ran over. Brynn fell into his arms. "I'm so happy you're okay," Dex murmured.

"I was so worried about you," Brynn said at the same time.

Dex held her at arm's length. There were red splotches on his cheeks, and his forehead was sweaty. "I don't think they saw me, but I'm not sure. Did you get a look at anyone?"

"I saw the guy who chased after you. It was the same guy who was interrogating me in my memory. I'm sure of it." She ran her hands up his arms. "It's a miracle he didn't find you. I swear you two were inches away from each other when you were hiding in that bush."

"I know." Dex swallowed nervously. "We're in over our heads. We have to take a step back, I think. If they figure out we're on to them, something awful could happen to us."

Brynn scoffed. "But we can't stop now! We're close to nailing Merriweather, maybe even figuring out who's in ACL! I can feel it!"

"They could *kill* us, Brynn. Those guys had *guns*. We need to rethink this."

"Have you forgotten there's still a bomb out there? And Cortexia isn't just hurting teenagers—it's *killing* them."

Dex flinched. "How do you know *that*?"

"Because of her." She wheeled around, gesturing to Lexi's treadmill, expecting her old friend to give Dex a weary finger-waggle and say, *Surprise!* She blinked, then noticed the front door to the gym slowly swishing closed.

Lexi was gone.

TWENTY-TWO

THE DAY OF THE LAUNCH

At eight A.M., Brynn stood at a busy bus stop in Georgetown, a hood pulled tightly around her head. At school, homeroom was starting. Mrs. Hyde would be taking roll, but Brynn wouldn't be there to answer to the call of her name. Eventually, the office would call her parents, and they'd be worried sick about where she was.

But she couldn't dwell on that right now. The launch was in less than twelve hours. She needed to get to Lowell—he was her last hope. She hadn't wanted to find him at home, but she'd run out of options. She just hoped he hadn't *really* gone on vacation and was instead hiding out in his house until the launch was over.

Her phone beeped. *Lexi?* Brynn wondered. She'd texted

her former friend quite a few times since yesterday, desperately wanting to talk. Lexi was still a target. Merriweather's goons would surely try to get to her again and inject her so she'd forget what she knew. She'd warned Lexi to stay home and keep the doors locked, but it would make her feel better if Lexi checked in.

The text was from Dex instead. *Where are you?*

Brynn slipped the phone back into her pocket without answering. She couldn't keep her promise to Dex to let this go. Hopefully, when this was over, he'd understand why she'd gone on alone.

The others waiting for the bus shifted their weight and checked their phones. A woman hefted a baby higher onto her hip. A man paused and looked at Brynn closely, and she shivered. She had her hood up and dark sunglasses over her eyes, but she still felt too visible. Finally, the man looked away. He was older, skinny, tattooed; he looked like he worked at a trendy brewery or something, not for a senator. Right?

There was a roar at the corner, and the bus came into view. The people waiting silently formed a line. The bus stopped at the curb, its door hissing open. As Brynn fished for her bus pass, she felt a hand on her shoulder. "Don't get on," said a male voice in her ear.

She froze. "Keep your hood up," the voice continued. "Don't make any sudden moves. But step away from the line right now and walk into the alley, nice and calm. Got it?"

Brynn's knees trembled with sudden adrenaline. She nodded faintly and stepped back from the bus. As she hurried toward the alleyway behind her, the man—she caught sight of a dark sweatshirt with a hood, similar to her own— stayed right with her, his hand still on her shoulder, hard. By the time the bus pulled away from the stop, she was in the shadows. Gone.

"Come on." The man pushed her to the other end of the alley and toward a waiting, running vehicle. "Get in, and don't make trouble." He shoved her headfirst into the backseat, and before she could wheel around and fight back, he'd locked the doors and hurried around to the driver's side.

"Please," Brynn whispered as they peeled away, cutting off several cars and veering through lanes of traffic. She tried to wrench the door open to escape, but it was childlocked. "Where are you taking me?" she cried. "Please don't inject me again. *Please*. What you're doing is wrong. Don't you understand that?"

"I'm not going to inject you," the driver said. "I'm trying to *help* you."

Brynn frowned. All she could see was his dark hood— his face was in shadow. But suddenly she recognized the voice.

"They were watching you," he went on. "Across the street from that bus. You should have known better, Brynn. And maybe I should have, too. I should have never given you that file."

"Dr. *Lowell*?" Brynn whispered.

He glanced at her in the rearview mirror, and sure enough, there were Dr. Lowell's wire-rimmed glasses under the hood. "Anyway, I think we lost them. The bus blocked their view. I'm taking you to school now, okay? You'll be safe there. And I don't want you to talk about any of this again."

Brynn balled up her fists. "No. I've been trying to reach you for days. I'm not getting out of this car until you talk to me."

Lowell's eyes shifted back and forth. "It's not safe. And if your mother finds out—"

Brynn stiffened. "You really think I care what my mother thinks? *You're* the one who helped me know everything. So obviously you're interested in the truth, too."

"It's come at too much of a cost."

Lowell did a sudden, sharp right turn onto a side street, throwing Brynn against the window. But she recovered quickly, hitching forward until she was almost next to him. "Look, you either talk to me now, or I'm going to tell how you tipped me off to that data in my mom's drawer."

He inhaled sharply. *Tell who?* she expected him to ask,

but he didn't. After a beat, he slammed on the accelerator, sending Brynn tumbling backward.

"Hey!" she screamed. Maybe she'd been wrong about all of this. How trustworthy was Lowell, really? If he was part of ACL, he was crazy enough to want to bomb something. Or what if he was some kind of double agent? Who knew what side he was on?

Lowell wrenched the wheel to the left, suddenly turning into a park. Up a gravel path, he found a deserted parking lot and stopped the car. He glanced around cagily, checking through the front window, then the back. Brynn did, too. There was no one around. She didn't even notice any birds in the trees.

Finally, he glanced at her in the rearview mirror. "Fine. Let's talk. Go."

Brynn swallowed hard, still rattled. "I know Cortexia causes teenagers to kill themselves. And you must, too. That's why you told me about that file, right? You wanted me to see those crossed-out results. You knew I'd make the connection that every blacked-out line was for a young patient."

Lowell stared down at the steering wheel, saying nothing.

"You knew I was injected, too. Were you there when it happened?"

Lowell's eyes widened. *"No!"* His voice was full of shock. "Absolutely not. But I knew ... well, I saw the change in you, and I had my suspicions." He stared out the window. "We had this same discussion in August, Brynn. Someone told you what happened with the teenagers. A young patient who'd been through the clinical trials, I believe."

"Yes. My friend Lexi Gates."

Lowell frowned, as if Brynn had just given the wrong answer to an easy equation, but he shrugged and kept going. "I told you to keep quiet about it, that we'd figure it out. But then you cut off all contact with me. I tried to reach out countless times, with no luck. Your mother mentioned you were having a hard time emotionally. I had a hunch what might have happened to you, but it was too scary to accept. Then I saw you in her office, reinvestigating things you already knew . . . and then later, at the investors' dinner, when you tried to corner me, I had to come to terms with the fact that you *had* been injected. Your memories had been erased."

Brynn's throat felt like it was closing. "Do you know who injected me?"

Lowell let his hands drop to his lap. His fingers entwined together tightly. "I'd rather not say."

"My mom, right?" Her voice shook. "You don't have to protect her."

The blood had drained from Lowell's face. His eyes widened. "Goodness, Brynn. *No.* Your mother has no idea about any of this."

Brynn scoffed. "Of course she does! She has to!"

He turned around to face her. In the dull morning light, his face looked lined, and there were bags under his eyes. It looked as though he hadn't slept in days. "Okay, she *did* know. She was the one who ran the trials for the teenagers. I had no idea about it—I didn't know before you told me. But you said you were going to speak to her as well. And the day after you and I met, your mother called a meeting with BioXin's board of directors. I asked her what it was all about, but she said it didn't concern me, only that Cortexia had some issues and we needed to delay the launch. She was pumped up, angry. Distracted, too. So I assumed she was going to report the results of those teenage patients. It's terribly dangerous to administer the Cortexia treatment to teenagers, as you know—especially teenagers already predisposed to depression. It's not like SSRI medications; instead of helping, it can actually send young patients into a dangerous shadow state where they aren't themselves anymore. They aren't in control of their actions. Their memories aren't theirs anymore. It's incredibly damaging to a young brain."

"Shadow state," Brynn whispered, feeling chills. "And then what happened?" she added, confused by this new development.

He pulled his glasses off and wiped them on his shirt. "Well, she had the meeting. It went very long—I didn't see her at all that day. The next morning, she came in and went to work as usual. She took meetings to plan the launch. I asked her if she was still concerned about Cortexia's flaws, and she looked at me like she had no idea what I was talking about."

A cold, slippery sensation washed over Brynn. "My mother was given Cortexia, too?"

"I think she must have been. And maybe your father as well." Anguish washed over Lowell's face. "I'm certain your mother talked Cortexia's problems over with him—I know how close they are. But when I next saw him, he seemed supportive of the medication."

The fights. All those slammed doors, those heated conversations. Brynn's parents were trying to figure out what to do about Cortexia. Dr. Caldwell had worked for years on it, and suddenly everything was going wrong. Of course it was trying for them. They'd banked everything on Cortexia. And now those dreams had exploded.

But then, right around when school started, the fog lifted, and everyone was happy again. *Oblivious* again. Her mom. Her dad. *Brynn.* They'd all been given Cortexia at the same time. They forgot their struggles.

She met Lowell's gaze. "Are you sure my mom doesn't know about this?"

Lowell frowned. "I know your mother would never, *ever* allow Cortexia to go out if she knew how it hurt young people—or anyone. She's been kept in the dark. I'm a hundred percent sure."

Brynn felt breathless. And also thrilled and relieved. Her mother was innocent! She *was* the good person Brynn had always known! But the feeling didn't last for long. She glanced at Lowell, panic rushing in again. "So who put those black lines through the data if it wasn't my mom?"

"BioXin. I don't know for sure, but I have friends in the archive department, and the day after the meeting, I went down and looked through some papers the board of directors were getting rid of. That's when I found that data with the slashes through it. I was never able to find the original file, and I was never able to see what was under those black lines, but just the fact that the company was trying to obliterate a clinical trial is incriminating."

"So why didn't you show it to the press? The FDA?"

"Because they would have just injected me, too. I needed to lie low. Wait for the appropriate time. I didn't even want the files in my office, so I decided to hide a copy of the files in your mom's filing cabinet, in that folder I told you about."

Brynn slumped against the backseat. This conversation was making her woozy. "But why is BioXin so desperate to roll out Cortexia, no matter what?"

"That's what confused me for so long. I thought it was just because of money—Cortexia is going to make BioXin a fortune. But it seemed to be about something beyond that. Something bigger, deeper. When I saw Merriweather at the investors' dinner, it fell into place." Lowell looked at her grimly, and Brynn could just tell, somehow, what he was going to say next. "I know Merriweather's politics. I know how desperate he is to wipe out terrorism, no matter the means. Cortexia is a powerful tool. It can alter people's minds, thoughts, *opinions.* It's the ultimate weapon."

There was an almost reverent silence as they both thought about this. Brynn swallowed hard. She'd come up with exactly the same theory, but it was sickening to hear Lowell say it aloud.

"But your mother holds the patent, and she keeps Cortexia's biochemical formula under wraps," Lowell went on. "Even *I'm* not sure of the full process of how it's produced—I deal more with the brain-mapping and MRI work. So BioXin and Merriweather need your mother onboard to continue making the chemical. And for that, she needs to remain ignorant of what they're up to. If she gets a whiff of something nefarious, she could walk—and take her formula with her. Or she could destroy the information and refuse to tell them how it's made."

"Would they come after her if she did that?"

Lowell nodded. "It's possible. But at the moment, injections with her own medicine work just as well."

Brynn swallowed hard. She had no idea what to say. This was even worse than she'd thought.

There was a heavy *crack* outside. Lowell shot up straight

and peered out each window. Brynn's heart banged. "Where did that come from?"

"I don't know, but I'm not taking any chances." Lowell started the car. "This is why it's very dangerous for us to be talking about this. They're *among* us, Brynn. *Watching.* They hear everything."

Brynn shivered, recalling the paranoid feelings that had overtaken her as she'd waited for the bus. But then those feelings turned to ones of frustration. "So we're supposed to hide the rest of our lives? We have to tell people about this. BioXin and Merriweather can't go forward with their plan! It's diabolical!"

"I know." Lowell looked both ways down the street, then turned into traffic. "That's why I've decided I'm going to go public with this. Today."

Brynn gasped. "Really?"

He nodded, zooming through a yellow light. "I've already put a call in to a reporter at CNN. I'm going to hold a press conference at five P.M. There will be a news blast everywhere. They can't inject the *whole* country. After that, the FDA will hopefully get involved. They'll cart away the medication. They'll protect the formula. Merriweather won't be able to get his hands on it."

"Wow," Brynn said, a thrill going through her. "That's ... amazing. But what about my mom? Are you going to tell her first?"

"Yes. I'm going to drive to the office now. It'll take a while to explain it to her. She's going to take it hard—same as she did last time she found out. But it's for the best, and she'll understand that."

With one hand, Lowell opened his glove box, pulled out a sheaf of rolled-up papers, and handed them to Brynn. It was the same lab results he'd told her about, the ones from the file in her mother's office. Brynn held them at arm's length, shocked.

"I made another copy," Lowell explained. "Just in case."

"And they're for *me*?"

He nodded. "Keep them safe. Don't show them to anyone, not even your boyfriend. I know you've been together for a long time, but the fewer people who know, the better. I hope you won't have to look at them after today, though. I hope everyone already knows the truth."

Brynn looked up at him. "So is it you? Are you ACL?"

Lowell's eyes narrowed into slits. "What's ACL?"

"The..." Brynn swallowed hard. Lowell wasn't lying. He really didn't know. Then again, maybe it didn't matter. If Lowell went public, the launch would be canceled. There would be no need for a bomb.

Lowell drove her all the way to school, letting her out close to a door and watching as she ran safely inside. Even after Brynn was in the school's warm downstairs hall, she still felt chilled to the bone. She knew she should feel satisfied after her talk with Lowell—and relieved, too. And she was . . . but something he'd just said didn't sit right. She worked his words over in her brain but couldn't figure out what it could be.

The hall was empty. Despite that, she pressed the papers Lowell had given her tightly to her chest and kept her eyes steady in front of her. As though she were hiding nothing. As though she wasn't someone who held an important secret in the palm of her hand.

TWENTY-THREE

Four forty-five P.M. Brynn was barely able to contain herself as she sat in front of the TV in Dex's den.

"What time did Lowell say he was giving the press conference again?" Dex murmured.

"Five," Brynn said.

Dex nodded. Brynn wanted to reach for his hand, but he'd been standoffish since they'd gotten here. He was upset that she'd gone behind his back and snuck off to see Lowell. He was worried, obviously, but didn't he realize Brynn had had no choice? Lowell had filled in a huge piece of the puzzle, and she'd been eager to tell Dex everything, intercepting him the moment the bell rang at school. Brynn was glad he'd ditched the rest of the day to meet her at his house. She needed him for protection.

"I'm just happy this is going to be over," Dex said. "The launch will be canceled. The bombing won't happen. The protest group will get what they need, too. Cortexia will go back to the drawing board. No one will suffer from it ever again."

"I know," Brynn said quietly. But then she felt a pang, thinking about her mom. It was strange she hadn't heard from her all day . . . but so much must be happening now that Lowell had revealed everything. Still, Brynn would have thought someone would have called her to say that the launch event was canceled. Maybe they'd forgotten about her in all the chaos?

Another commercial came on television, and Brynn gritted her teeth. She wished Lowell would make the announcement already. Jittery, she glanced around the room, eager for something to focus on to pass the next few minutes. They didn't spend much time at Dex's place—he claimed it was hard to be here, as every piece of furniture, every picture on the wall reminded him of Marc. And it was true: The den was a Marc shrine. There were pictures of him on the football team. In a tuxedo, on his way to the prom. In a graduation cap and gown, and then in his military uniform. His Medal of Honor was housed in a frame and hung on the wall. A triangular folded flag from his funeral sat in a wooden case on the mantel.

Brynn scanned the photographs tucked into the little nooks on the media console, noting that, for once, these *weren't* of Marc. There was one of Dex's parents at a wedding, his dad in a tuxedo, looking like an older version of Dex, his mom's eyes twinkling like Marc's. Another was of Dex in midair, leg extended, kicking a soccer ball into a goal. And there was Dex's school photo from this year, which they'd only received a few weeks ago. It was nice to see that the Kinsleys put up memorabilia for themselves and their other son, the one who was still alive. Sometimes it seemed like Marc overshadowed Dex even in death.

Something else was tucked behind Dex's school picture. Brynn squinted. It seemed to be a small white square. She'd seen something like it before. She uncurled her hand from Dex's and walked over to it.

"What are you doing?" Dex asked.

"What is that?" Brynn murmured, about to grab the card from behind the photos.

"Wait, look!"

He was pointing at the TV. The newscast had come back on, and the words BIOXIN LABS ANNOUNCEMENT scrolled across the screen. Brynn turned back. Her stomach did a flip. Here it was.

She scuttled back to the couch and sat down. A news anchor stood in front of the BioXin building, saying that an official at BioXin was going to make a "major announcement."

"BioXin's newest and most promising medication, Cortexia, is having its launch to the public tonight," the reporter said. "Quite a few celebrities and Washington insiders will be attending, as well as the soldiers who were in the drug's early clinical trials for PTSD and who saw dramatic—almost miraculous—improvements."

"That's not all that happened," Brynn muttered, nervously picking at the skin on the side of her thumb.

"Ah, here comes someone now," the reporter said, glancing over her shoulder.

Brynn expected to see Lowell shuffling out of the building in his lab coat and loosened tie, but it was someone else, a slick-looking man she recognized from the investors' dinner, wearing a well-cut suit. The man strode up to the reporter and shook her hand. "This is Bruce Cress, CEO of BioXin Labs," the reporter trilled.

Dex gave Brynn a cautious smile. "Did Lowell mention involving BioXin's CEO?"

"No . . . ," Brynn said, an uneasy feeling twisting in her gut.

Bruce Cress thanked the reporter. He stepped to the microphone and began to speak, his voice smooth and commanding. "As you know, BioXin labs has been making great strides in its development of Cortexia, an injectable medication that counteracts the ravaging effects of post-traumatic stress disorder. It was developed by esteemed scientists Dr. Celeste Caldwell and Dr. Alfred Lowell, who have worked tirelessly to produce a medication that can restore our returning soldiers after the stress of battle."

Brynn's heart swished in her ears. Just hearing Lowell's name gave her a jolt.

"I have two announcements," Cress said, giving the camera a broad smile. "The first is that we've completed our five-year findings from the first Cortexia clinical trial as of today. I'm proud to report that not only were one hundred percent of the soldiers relieved of their PTSD symptoms, but five years later, they still show no signs of relapse, mental illness, or any sort of mental strife compared to those in our control group. We at BioXin believe that not only is Cortexia a valuable medication, it's also a valuable tool for national security."

"*What?*" Brynn shot to her feet. "Where the hell is Lowell?"

Cress faced the camera again. There was something about those cold, ice-blue eyes that suddenly sparked something deep inside her. She was so shocked she dropped back to the couch like a stone. Of course, Cress was one of the men in her memory. He was the one who had asked her again and again what she knew and what she'd told.

"My second announcement is that, as part of our initiative to spread Cortexia far and wide, Senator Robert Merriweather of Virginia has promised to push through legislation that will allow all soldiers reporting from battle who suffer from symptoms of post-traumatic stress disorder to receive Cortexia at little to no cost," the CEO continued. "BioXin is proud to donate our services to the armed forces, and it's our hope that our medication can improve lives in a significant way that has never been seen before. Senator Merriweather couldn't be with us this afternoon, but we owe him a debt of gratitude."

The reporter began to chatter. An offscreen audience applauded. Brynn couldn't listen to this anymore. Her body burned with rage. She dialed the number to the lab. "Is Dr. Lowell in today?" she barked when the receptionist answered. Had they sent him on vacation permanently? Had they *killed* him?

"Who may I ask is calling?" the receptionist chirped.

Brynn wanted to crush the receiver. "Just get him for me if he's there!"

The receptionist told her to hold, and then the phone was ringing again. She was surprised when Lowell answered in a friendly, chipper voice. "This is Dr. Lowell!"

"It's Brynn," she said impatiently. "What's going on?"

There was a long pause. For a moment, Brynn wondered if they'd been disconnected. Then Lowell said, "I'm sorry. Brynn who?"

"Brynn Caldwell!" Brynn cried. "From this morning? You ambushed me at the bus stop?" But then a crack opened in her brain. There was only one reason why he wouldn't remember that.

Her grip on the phone loosened. She stared at Dex in resignation. She suddenly felt scooped out, empty.

"Oh, Celeste's daughter!" Lowell was still on the line. He sounded confused. "Are you looking for your mom? I believe she's in a meeting right now. Putting some finishing touches on her launch speech for tonight!"

Brynn's skin felt cold. When had they grabbed him? Right after they'd spoken? But *how*? Lowell had taken so many precautions to keep their conversation private, and to drop her off without being seen. Were the people at BioXin mind readers? Maybe there was a mole at CNN?

She hit End without telling Lowell good-bye, terrified that someone had recorded the whole conversation. By the way Dex was staring at her, it was pretty clear he'd figured out what had happened.

"*Shit,*" he whispered. "Cortexia?"

Brynn pressed her hands to her forehead. The reporter was still on TV in front of the BioXin building. A big headline blared at the bottom: CORTEXIA FIVE-YEAR OUTCOMES EVEN BETTER THAN EXPECTED. It was propaganda.

She looked at her phone again. "This has to be why Lowell gave me the data—maybe he suspected this was going to happen." She touched her bag, where she'd tucked the papers. Then she glanced out the window, half expecting to see a black car parked at the curb—someone keeping tabs on her. If Lowell was being watched, then so was she.

But why hadn't someone grabbed her, shut her down? Did they not yet know the extent of what she knew?

Suddenly that felt like an advantage. She had to spread the news before it was too late. "I'll call my mom," she said. "If Lowell didn't tell her, I will."

Dex shook his head. "They're probably tapping her phone. As soon as you tell the truth, they'll grab her and inject her—and you, too. It was probably a risk even to call Lowell just now."

"But we have to do *something*. Send this out ourselves. Post it on Twitter. Instagram. Snapchat. People need to *know* about this, Dex. This needs to be stopped."

"I agree," Dex said cautiously. "But social media can be deleted. Hacked. BioXin will just see it and take it down."

"So we hire a skywriter," Brynn said, not exactly kidding. "We paint it on a billboard."

"Let me just think." Dex stared at the ceiling. "I made some friends at the NSA. Good guys, honest guys. People who hate Merriweather and would detest something like this. I can scan this stuff and send it to them anonymously. They'll know what to do with it."

"Fine," Brynn agreed. "Let's do it now."

Dex's blue eyes were steady. "Okay."

Brynn's phone beeped, interrupting them. She stared down at it and almost laughed aloud. Her mother had texted. *We are leaving for the launch in an hour. You need to come home and get ready. Is Dex still coming as your date?*

Brynn shut her eyes. It hurt that her mom still didn't know. "We can't go," she whispered. "We can't pretend everything is fine. And also, what if I go and they inject me *there*?"

"They wouldn't take that risk, I don't think," Dex said. "We have to go. Keep up appearances. And anyway, being there, we'll be able to scope out the bomb situation."

Brynn squeezed her eyes shut. *The bomb.* Whoever the ACL was, they might still be ready to set it off. She suddenly felt angry. "God, I almost wish it would just happen. Maybe they could detonate it somewhere where they'd only get Merriweather and Cress."

Dex flinched. An uneasy look crossed his features. "Wait—you aren't serious, are you?"

"Of course not," Brynn said quickly. "I'm just frustrated. BioXin is in on this. The government is in on this. Who knows, maybe even the police are, too!"

Dex looked wary of her again, as though she were a feral dog he didn't want to touch. She shut her eyes, cursing the slip. "I know the police aren't, okay? But it's so frustrating. Call your NSA guys now. We're running out of time."

Dex glanced back into the TV room, but his gaze wasn't on the screen. Brynn turned to see what he was looking at, but he quickly faced her again. "Okay," he said warily.

He leaned over his phone and punched in the number.

After a moment, his eyes met hers. "Hello?" he said into the phone. "Yes, this is Mr. Avery's office? Um, yeah, I have documents I'd like to scan and send over for his review. . . ."

Brynn listened as he explained about the bomb and its location. In less than a minute, it was all over. Dex hung up silently, not meeting her eye. On the TV, the broadcast had switched to commercials again. Outside, a garbage truck rumbled past. "Well, okay," Brynn said. "What now?"

"I need to go scan these," Dex said, holding up the papers. "You go get ready for the launch. I'll see you there."

Brynn nodded. She stood on her tiptoes to kiss him. He returned the kiss limply and demurely, with no passion. Brynn's breath caught, but before she could assure him that she was still the person he'd always known, he hurried her out the door.

TWENTY-FOUR

B rynn stood in front of her mirror, touching the red silk dress she'd bought for the launch many months before. The fabric was so thin and soft, it almost felt like a feather gently caressing her skin. As she twirled, the skirt flared out flirtatiously. With her hair curled and a slash of pink lipstick, she looked more grown-up than ever, and she could almost pass as the buoyantly happy daughter of the night's biggest star. Only her eyes, dark, black-circled, narrowed with worry, gave her away. That and her trembling hands.

She looked down at her phone. She expected some kind of alert to come through—from her anonymous texter, maybe—shaming her for alerting the authorities. But there was nothing. Nor had anyone burst into her house to inject her. And though Dex had texted her a few times, his messages were terse, unemotional. It was worrying...for so many reasons. Did he really not trust her? What if he was going to turn *her* in, too?

She pushed the thought from her mind. Dex wouldn't do that. Still, something was making her uneasy, unsettled. She couldn't put her finger on it.

Then again, maybe it was everything.

The door creaked, and Brynn whirled around. Her mother stepped in, dressed in a fitted black dress and dramatically high heels. Her hair cascaded down her back in wavy curls, and she smelled like lilacs. "Whoa," Brynn breathed, momentarily forgetting everything between them.

"Honey," Dr. Caldwell breathed at the same time as she took Brynn in, "you look amazing."

Brynn felt a pang. "You do, too," she said softly.

"Are you ready for tonight?" Dr. Caldwell reached out and pushed a lock of hair out of Brynn's eyes. "I know things haven't been great between us."

Brynn felt a lump in her throat. She felt terrible for doubting her mom for even a second. Her mother wasn't hiding anything. She'd been given Cortexia, too.

"I'm sorry," she said. "My attitude, the things I've said... let's just forget about it."

Dr. Caldwell cocked her head. "But I don't want to

forget. That you could believe I'd be unscrupulous with my research—Brynn, I would *never*."

"I know." Suddenly, Brynn felt a bolt of fear. "Wait, you didn't share what I said with anyone, did you?"

Her mother shook her head. "No. I wanted to talk to you about it first. But what gave you the idea that I'd lied about Cortexia? Did someone say something?"

"I—I got mixed up," Brynn stammered, blurting out the first thing that came to mind. Hopefully, she'd dodged a bullet. If her mother had voiced concerns about Cortexia, she would have been injected all over again—or maybe even worse. "I'm really, really sorry."

"Well, I'm sorry I didn't tell you about Harvard until recently," Dr. Caldwell admitted. "I should have been honest. Maybe I *was* trying to be perfect around you. And then, when you got so angry, I was afraid you'd lost all respect for me."

Brynn shook her head. "I was shocked when you told me." Tears filled her eyes. "But you made a mistake when you were young." She swallowed a lump in her throat. "There's a difference between making a mistake and being a terrible person. And you are *not* a terrible person."

Dr. Caldwell's eyes welled, too. "Oh, honey," she said, then moved in for a hug. Brynn squeezed her tightly, so thrilled to have her mother back. Then her mom stepped away and looked at her. "So what *was* going on at the office the other day? Why were you there?"

Brynn breathed in. Here was her chance to tell her mom about Cortexia. It was terrible timing, yes, and she felt so sad—her mother's medication, her pride and joy, wasn't going to be celebrated. But telling her was the right thing to do.

"Actually—" she started. But then the doorbell rang.

Her mom's eyes lit up, and she walked to the window. A black limo sat in the driveway. "It's for us, for the launch!" she cried. "And guess who we're riding with?"

"Dad?" Brynn asked, her heart still pounding hard.

"*Obviously*," her mom said. "But also Bruce Cress, BioXin's CEO. That's a *huge deal*, Brynn. He doesn't make time for anyone."

Brynn froze. Her interrogator . . . in the driveway? She stared at the idling limo. There was no way she could tell her mom now. Cress would *know*. He would sense something was off with her mother, and who knew, maybe he'd inject them in the backseat. And then they would go to the launch knowing nothing, and Merriweather could do whatever he liked with Cortexia. Or the bomb might go off, and hundreds could be dead.

She stepped back and searched her mother's face. Dr. Caldwell looked so excited. This was the pinnacle of her career. The secret inside Brynn swelled, begging to be told, but she held her tongue. "Th-That's great," she said. Because what else *could* she say?

Her mother fiddled with something in her hands, and

Brynn looked down. Her mother held several small cards with the BioXin logo displayed on the top. Brynn straightened up. She'd seen that same card at Dex's house. "What are those?" she asked.

Dr. Caldwell smiled. "Oh. They're for soldiers who recently came home. I figured there might be some guys in the audience tonight who might be interested in contacting us."

Brynn ran her finger over the top card's embossed surface. "Are they new?" She'd never seen them before—well, besides earlier today.

Her mother shook her head. "Oh, no. I've been giving them out for about a year and a half now. I just don't usually have any on me. It's typically other people on the team who distribute them, but Cress asked that I give out some personally tonight."

"They're nice," Brynn said, feeling uneasy. *Really* uneasy. "A-And do most of the soldiers contact you, after you give them one of these cards?"

"Most of them, yes." Her mother dropped the little cards into her clutch. "I mean, wouldn't you, if you had PTSD? It's not like people want to live with it."

That was what Brynn was afraid of. She felt numb, suddenly. Boneless. "Um, can I have a minute to myself?" she squeaked out, fully aware that beads of sweat had just broken out on her forehead. "I'm having a bra malfunction."

"Be quick, okay?" Her mother patted Brynn's head. "I don't want to keep Cress waiting."

Brynn listened to her footsteps padding down the hall. Then she turned to her room and stared at her furniture. Her head felt hot. Spots passed in front of her eyes. *It might not be what you think,* she told herself. Dex might have taken a BioXin card when they ransacked her mom's office. He could have pulled one from Lowell's manila folder when Brynn wasn't looking.

But why would he put it *there,* in his family's den? There was only one reason, and she knew it. The force of the realization was almost palpable, like a shove to her chest. She found herself drooping to her mattress. *It's hard to hang around this house too much,* Dex always told her. *There are too many memories of Marc.*

What else would Brynn find about Marc if she looked around Dex's house more thoroughly? Was there something Dex didn't *want* her to know?

Marc was part of the trial. Brynn was suddenly sure of it with every cell in her body, every ounce of her heart. He'd come back from Afghanistan haunted and changed. Someone at BioXin had given him a card. And of course he'd called them, just like her mother said. Of course he wanted to feel better.

But he'd been only nineteen at the time, and as far as Brynn had known, her mother didn't test people that young, which was why she'd never asked Dex if Marc had tried the medication. But she'd been wrong. Marc must still have been under the cutoff age where Cortexia had a different effect on the brain . . . and Cortexia made him worse, not better. That tumble Marc had taken into the gorge? Maybe it wasn't an accident. Maybe Cortexia *made* him do that, just as it had altered Brynn's brain, practically forcing her into the water a few days before.

Marc had been given Cortexia, and it had killed him. And Dex knew this. He *had* to know. It all seemed so obvious, suddenly. Marc's death being an accident was just the official report. Perhaps it was even something his parents chose to believe. But Dex knew Marc best. He knew what his brother would and wouldn't do. He knew that his brother ended his life on purpose . . . and he knew a little chemical swimming through his system was to blame.

But did Dex know that *she* knew this? Did he realize she'd put together that the card in his den was a card from the clinical trial? Brynn thought about how Dex had glanced toward the den right before she left. Maybe he was looking at the card, making a mental note to put it away after she was gone. So was *he* ACL, then? Brynn could certainly see his motivation. Cortexia murdered his brother and then buried the evidence! And now to find out there was a government plot to use the medication in counterterrorism? No doubt he was disgusted, and for even deeper reasons now.

And had he been the one texting her? Brynn tried the idea on for size. But why wouldn't Dex want her to know his identity? Why wouldn't he have immediately filled her in after her memory was lost, telling her what she'd been fighting for? *Did* he know about the bomb...and want it to go off?

Calm down, she told herself. She hadn't even *known* Dex when she'd drawn that schematic for the bomb. Someone else had talked her into that. Besides, Dex didn't want to bomb anything—he wanted to *stop* the bombing. That was what he'd been saying all along. He'd even called the authorities.

Right? But suddenly, she wasn't sure. Maybe he was going to strap the thing to his body and run through the atrium, screaming out the truth. Brynn thought of the pain that rocked Dex's face whenever he visited his brother at the cemetery. Dex might be capable of something like that. He might see it as a way to honor Marc. He was coming from a good place, a hurting place, but it was crazy that he thought violence was the answer.

Legs shaking, Brynn got to her feet and smoothed down her dress. Sun streamed through the window and spilled across her waist, splicing her half in light, half in shadow. All of a sudden, she felt calm and in control. She knew everything now. The world seemed clear after so many months of darkness. She folded the map of the BioXin building she'd printed from the USB stick and tucked it into her clutch. She was going to need it. She was going to find this bomb—and Dex—no matter what.

TWENTY-FIVE

"Oh, Celeste," Bruce Cress cooed as the family stepped into the atrium that evening. "This is just beautiful. You should be so proud."

Brynn's mother ducked her head. "I wasn't the decorator. But yes, it looks nice, doesn't it?" She laughed nervously and fiddled with the diamond bracelet on her wrist—a gift from the BioXin board of directors.

Brynn followed the group into the atrium, silently glowering at the CEO's back. The ride to BioXin in the same limo as her interrogator had been torturous. Every glance he'd sent her way, every evil chuckle—it all made her skin crawl. But as far as she could tell, he hadn't guessed the extent of what she knew or remembered. It had been nearly impossible not to lose it—especially given what she'd realized about Marc and Dex—but she'd kept it together.

Photographers were snapping pictures of people as they stepped through the doors. A string quartet was playing a Bach concerto in the corner. The space smelled like fresh flowers and gourmet food, and waiters were dashing around with trays of cocktails and canapés. A crowd even larger than she'd expected crammed the atrium so thickly she could barely walk. Her nostrils twitched at the heady mix of different colognes and perfumes, and everywhere she turned, she saw someone she recognized—famous journalists, senators and congressmen, scientists whose work she'd long admired, and even the secretary of defense. Dr. Lowell was here, too, looking polished in a tuxedo. He stood next to Martin, her mom's assistant, telling a joke. His cheeks shone. His eyes gleamed. *He has no idea,* Brynn thought. BioXin had gotten him, and they'd gotten him good.

"Where's Dex?" her father murmured, turning to Brynn.

Brynn tried to smile, though she had a feeling it looked more like a grimace. "Um, I'm sure he'll be along soon!" she said brightly. She scanned the upper levels that overlooked the atrium. Where would he hide a bomb? Somewhere where it would do a lot of damage . . . or somewhere just to make a point? She shut her eyes. She still couldn't believe Dex was involved in such a thing. *Maybe someplace just to prove a point,* she thought again. Because he didn't want to hurt anyone, right? He just wanted to scare people? To make people see the truth?

Still, she couldn't take the risk.

She noticed guards at the doors, and one by the elevator bank. No bomb down here, then. On which floor upstairs? An area right over the podium would inflict massive damage . . . but it was so out in the open, with nowhere to hide something bomblike. And yet, it had to be somewhere accessible without a keycard or office ID—a door with a breakable lock, maybe, as opposed to a door with sensors that responded to a fingerprint ID or a card-swipe, like her mother's lab, way down on the far end of the second floor, just visible from where she was standing. Brynn quickly scanned all the doors with proper knobs that she could see. A supply closet? The elevator shaft? Or what about the elevator machinery room? It stood right next to the elevators on the second floor, just above where one of the bars had been set up. It was loud in there, and cramped, and probably easily accessible. . . .

But what was she supposed to do, find it herself? That seemed impossible—and terrifying. Suddenly, something hit her. Dex obviously hadn't contacted the NSA or anyone else . . . but she could. Right now. It might mean she'd be injected on-site, but at least the authorities could protect everyone, *do* something about this.

She pulled her phone from her bag. Her fingers shook as she dialed 911. But as she put the phone to her ear, it didn't ring. She frowned at the screen. There was no cell service or wireless access, which was bizarre; three days ago, when she'd visited the atrium with her parents, she'd had four bars.

At that same moment, her mother turned to her with a dazzling smile. "Honey, I want to introduce you to someone. Come with me."

"But...," Brynn started, though her mother was already pulling her through the crowd. They passed soldiers in their dress military uniforms. They'd brought their young wives and children. Every soldier who passed touched Brynn's mother's arm and thanked her profusely. Dr. Caldwell stopped and spoke to each of them in turn, kissing cheeks and introducing Brynn. Brynn smiled politely, but she couldn't bear to make conversation. These men, just a few years older than Marc had been, were smiling, laughing, talking. They looked happy and relaxed, their demons extracted from their heads. She thought of the one photo of Marc she'd seen after he'd returned from Afghanistan, his eyes shifty, the corners of his mouth turned down, a look of permanent worry etched across his face. It wasn't fair. Cortexia had cured these guys, but it had sent Marc into the depths of hell.

Marc. She glanced around for Dex, half expecting to see him crouched in the corner with a bomb strapped to his body. The thought made her throat close. It was impossible. Unthinkable. A nightmare. This was her boyfriend, someone she thought she knew inside and out—and he'd *lied* to her. But she couldn't dwell on that right now. She needed to find Dex, settle him down, make sure he was safe. She glanced around the huge space, paying careful attention to the nooks and crannies on the upper level that overlooked the atrium. Then she checked the entrance again. There were a few security guards on-site, but certainly no one from the bomb squad. Dex clearly hadn't called them. That only solidified her hunch that he wanted the bombing to go as planned.

As her mother stopped to speak to yet another soldier, Brynn touched her shoulder. "I have to go outside for a sec, okay?"

"Hold on," her mother said, her eyes on someone a few steps away. "*There* you are!" A figure glided toward her. When Brynn saw who it was, she sucked in a breath. Merriweather.

The senator and Brynn's mom embraced. Then Dr. Caldwell wrapped an arm around Brynn and ushered her forward. "Senator, this is my daughter, Brynn. She's a huge fan."

Up close, the senator's skin was flawless, and his teeth were almost too white. He had a chiseled, rakish face framed by dark, thick eyebrows and soulful gray eyes. He wore a well-fitted, expensive-looking navy suit with a tiny American flag pin on the lapel, but despite all of this, there seemed to be something dirty about him. As he looked at Brynn, his eyebrows shot up playfully. "Is that so?" he asked. "And why are you such a fan, Miss Caldwell?"

He knows, Brynn thought with a start. Then again, of *course* he did. The senator had been in the room when she was injected. He'd ordered the gray Corolla to follow her around. But was he aware of how much of her memory had returned? She hoped not.

Her mother nudged her, and Brynn realized she was supposed to answer. She looked at the senator again. He had such a smug look on his face, as though Brynn were a cornered bug he was about to squash. *He's using you!* She wanted to scream at her mom. *He doesn't care about Cortexia treating PTSD—he wants to get his hands on it so he can mind-control suspected terrorists—and maybe the whole country!* She balled her hands into fists, wishing she could punch him. No wonder Dex was angry. She *got* it.

Something behind her shifted. A guy in a black suit and sunglasses loomed close, his eyes seemingly locked on her. A tough-looking woman glanced over her shoulder from a conversation nearby, on alert. How many people in this room were clued in to the senator's schemes? How many would tackle her the moment she ran out of the building, desperate for cell service, desperate to call the cops?

But she couldn't just stand here, either. If she couldn't call the police, then she had to move on to plan B. Her eyes dropped to the floor. "Um, it's nice to meet you," she mumbled, hating herself for saying even that.

The moment she could get away from them, she did. It took her a few minutes to get to the other side of the atrium. She looked around to make sure no one was watching. The coast seemed clear. She ducked into a small hallway that was out of the party scene and pulled out the building schematic, carefully assessing the circled doorways and exits. Her gaze swept the upper level. Several cameras slowly panned the scene, which gave her pause. Hadn't Dex told her the building manager said none of the cameras worked? Or was that yet another lie? Had he not wanted her to see the camera footage because he knew *he'd* be in it?

She felt her throat contract, shattered all over again by Dex's duplicity. *Hold it together. You can fall apart later.* She squared her shoulders and looked at the building map once more. Perhaps Dex had hidden the bomb somewhere, then run.

The elevator machinery room. It had to be. None of the other locations made any sense.

There was a stairwell behind her that led to the second floor. Heart pounding, she climbed the rickety steps, careful not to trip in her shoes. A door opened onto the second level. Office doors were on one side, a railing that overlooked the atrium on the other. Brynn glanced over the balcony, catching sight of her mother's dark, sleek head. She'd moved back to the soldiers and was pinching a baby's cheek.

Brynn spied Senator Merriweather whispering something to Bruce Cress. Brynn's hand clenched into a fist. They both looked so satisfied. Their plan had gone swimmingly. Soon they'd have enough Cortexia to do whatever they wanted, and BioXin was probably going to make a fortune from its top-secret government contract. It wasn't right. It wasn't *fair*.

The elevator's mechanical room was to her left. Tiptoeing there, Brynn twisted the cold metal knob and was surprised when the door easily opened. Someone had broken the lock. This was it.

She took a deep breath and peered inside. Various generators hummed. Lights blinked. It took a moment for her eyes to adjust, and she braced herself for a surprise. But nothing happened. As far as she could tell, it just looked like elevator mechanicals. Brynn blinked, thinking of the pictures of bombs she'd seen in books that they'd discussed in physics class. She didn't see any wires extending from dynamite sticks. She didn't see any digital countdown clocks. The bomb wasn't here. How was this possible?

She shut the door and stood outside the room, trying to think. Maybe Dex had realized she'd found him out. Maybe he'd backed off the whole operation. Or perhaps he really had gotten in touch with his NSA contact and they were handling this instead, nonviolently.

Something flashed at the end of the hall, just beyond the door to her mother's office. Brynn stood straighter. *Dex?* Whoever it was had his broad shoulders and strong jaw. She tiptoed toward the figure, trying to stick close to the wall so no one at the party would notice her up here. The doors to her mother's lab stood open at the very end of the hallway, which was unusual; on a night like tonight, with a lot of people in the atrium, she'd figured no one would be working.

But a single light shone inside the lab.

She ran down the hall toward the lab. Brynn swallowed hard. The lab door stood open. The light still shone from inside. "Dex?" she called out softly, her voice immediately swallowed up by the din below. "Dex?" she called again as she moved closer. All of a sudden, she felt like she might cry.

She touched the door, too afraid to go farther. She sensed a presence inside, though, maybe listening. "Dex, if that's you, I understand why you're doing this," she said. "I'm mad that you lied to me, but I know how Marc's death destroyed you, and if it's because of Cortexia ... well, I don't blame you for being angry. What they're covering up isn't fair. What Merriweather and Cress are doing is disgusting. I want them gone, too."

Something seemed to shift around the corner. Brynn swore she heard a sigh. Tears streamed down her cheeks. "And I forgive you," she whispered. "I know you're a good person. I know you have good intentions. And I'm still *on your side*. But just come out, okay? Come out and let's talk about this."

There was still no answer. Mustering up her courage, she pushed the door open with a creak. The lab was dark and cool. She looked around but saw nothing. The door to the medication storage facility stood to her right. Brynn took a step toward it. "Dex?" she whispered. "Dex!"

A small window provided a view into the storage area. Brynn peered through, expecting to see Dex there, but all she saw were refrigerators and rows and rows of shelves. Then something on the ground caught her eye, and she sucked in a breath. It was a small, octagonal object with wires sticking out every which way. A small red light blinked frantically. A cold sweat broke out on her skin. She knew what it was.

"Dex?" Brynn whispered. "Dex!"

No answer. She stared again at the blinking bomb. Should she call the police herself? But what would she say? How would she explain how she found this? She couldn't incriminate herself... but she couldn't incriminate Dex, either. Despite everything, she still loved him so much.

There was only one answer. She needed to get this thing out of here herself. *Now.*

TWENTY-SIX

Brynn reached for the knob on the door to the storage room, but it didn't twist. To the right was a keypad softly glowing under an LED light. Brynn stared at it in frustration, totally at a loss as to what the code might be. Was it something her mother set? A four-digit combo only she'd know?

Frantically, she keyed in her mom's birthday. An angry *beep* blared out, blazing through her like an electric shock. Gathering her courage, she tried her own birthday next. Another rejection. She clasped her hands to her chest, afraid that if she tried once more, the keypad would lock down and set off some sort of alarm. Or would it be *good* to set off an alarm? Brynn thought of the security guards looming downstairs. If they came up here and found her with the bomb, would they know she'd been the one who designed it? What if this got *her* in trouble, somehow—or Dex? But she couldn't just leave it here. It would kill everyone.

She looked at the keypad again and racked her brain. For her ATM code, the garage code, and most of the passwords on her computer, her mother used Alois Alzheimer's birthday: 0614. It was her last shot. Holding her breath, she typed it in, deciding that if an alarm sounded, she would run. For a moment, there was only silence. Then the hollow, metallic *click* of a lock releasing. *"Thank you, Brynn Caldwell,"* said an automated voice. The words rang in Brynn's ears. How did the computer know she'd been the one to key that in? Could it *see* her, somehow?

She pushed the door open and refrigerated air wafted against her face. The bomb on the ground looked slick and shiny, like a beetle. Brightly colored wires snaked spaghetti-like from a bunch of ports. A digital timer reading 5:00 sat in the center. Just looking at it, Brynn suddenly had a flash of memory, of arranging those wires in a neat row on a table. *Pulling this one will deactivate it,* she explained to someone, pointing to one of the wires. She pointed to another. *Pulling this one will increase the timer.* And another: *Pulling this will cause no consequence. But pulling this one*—and here she pointed to the final color—*will cause it to instantly explode.*

She *had* built the bomb. She pinched the bridge of her

nose, trying to remember more of the specific details—like what color wire would increase the timer or make the thing explode. And also, who had she been talking to? It felt like it was someone she cared about. Someone with whom she was almost flirting.

She leaned down to inspect the device. Someone had written *This End Up* next to the timer. It seemed like a silly thing to Brynn—wasn't it obvious that the timer would have to face up, so you'd know how much time was left until it detonated?—but this, too, sparked another buried memory. *If you're confused, just write* This End Up *on the top,* she'd joked. Whoever it was had nudged her back. *In the same way people put those "fragile" stickers on boxes containing china plates, right?* She'd winked. *Right, smart cookie.*

The person in the half dream did as he was told, slowly writing *This End Up* with a silver Sharpie marker. There was something about the peculiar way whoever it was wrote his *S,* though, with a little extraneous loop at the bottom, that gave her pause. Brynn looked hard at it, her nose practically kissing the device. She thought of the love letters in the shoebox, the ones she'd just looked through a few days ago. It was uncanny. Jacob made his *S* the very same way.

So Jacob *had* been the one she'd been talking to. His email to her, the one saying he was in Colorado, was a lie. Was it Jacob who'd put the bomb here, and not Dex at all?

Without warning, nausea overtook her, and she had to take a deep breath to keep from throwing up. What did

Jacob want with protesting Cortexia? And how on earth had he convinced her to build a bomb? A peal of laughter from the party broke her out of her speculation. She glanced at the door, hoping the police would arrive. Maybe Dex *had* called them after all. Maybe all her musings about him were dead wrong. She *hoped* so.

But the party continued apace. The security guards patrolled the doors, looking bored. And Dex was still nowhere to be seen.

Brynn crouched down and picked up the small, square device. It felt eerily cool in her hands. Multicolored wires jutted and curled from every angle. When she lifted it, it was heavier than she expected, and her muscles strained under its weight. As her fingers adjusted to get a better grip, there was an electronic *bloop,* and suddenly a portion of the device lit up. Brynn froze. The spot under her thumb glowed a bright, toxic green. When she moved her thumb away, her print remained behind, luminescent in the dark room.

Device Activated, read the small digital screen. And then, suddenly, the clock began to click down. *Four fifty-nine, four fifty-eight.*

Brynn's mouth dropped open. Her thumbprint had set things into motion. And just like that, another memory slotted into place, mocking her. *We're only doing this as an exercise,* she heard herself say as she fitted the bomb's last pieces into place. She held up a small, flat electronic panel. *Just to make sure, I'm using my thumbprint as the only key that can unlock this thing. No one else can set it off, only me. Which means it's never going to go off. Not as long as I live.*

She smiled at someone across the table. It *was* Jacob. There he was in her memory, crisp and clear. He smirked back in that way he had. *I think that's smart,* he said. *We don't want anyone to do anything foolish.*

Spots formed in front of Brynn's eyes. She felt like she might faint. She was the only one who could activate this thing, and here she'd done it unwittingly. Had her memory been intact, of course she would have never picked the bomb up. She would have called the cops. They would have all been safe. But Jacob knew this weakness about the device. He'd slowly given her information about the bomb, knowing she'd go looking for it—and that she'd touch it, try to disarm it. She was as much a tool in this diabolical plan as the bomb was. She was the pulled pin in the grenade. The bullet in the gun.

Her breathing quickened. She couldn't leave the bomb here. It would destroy everyone. But she couldn't get it out of the building in time, either. She was stuck.

Four thirty-nine. Four thirty-eight. The numbers blurred in front of Brynn's eyes. She studied the wires. Which deactivated the bomb? Why couldn't she remember?

"Brynn!"

She was so startled that she nearly dropped the bomb on her toe. Turning her head, she anticipated seeing Jacob—or perhaps Dex. When she saw Lexi, she let out a small scream.

Lexi stepped forward. Unlike everyone else at the party, she was wearing a sweatshirt and jeans and a black cap pulled over her head. She looked confused to find Brynn alone. "I've been trying to call you, but your phone keeps going to voice mail. There's something I need to—" she started, taking a step toward Brynn.

"Don't come any closer!" Brynn bellowed.

Lexi stopped. "W-Why?"

Brynn turned around fully, showing her the bomb. Lexi paled. Her mouth dropped open. She staggered backward, bumping into the wall. "Oh my God."

Brynn stared down at the bomb. It felt alive in her hands. There were only four minutes left until it went off. "I—I just found it here," she begged. "I swear."

Lexi's tongue flicked across her lips. All of a sudden, she didn't look afraid anymore—or even that surprised. "I know," she finally said. And then she extended her hand. "Come on. I can help."

TWENTY-SEVEN

Brynn sprinted as fast as she could across the hallway, the sound of her shoes ringing sharply off the hard walls and ceiling. She feared every step she took would be her last. She looked down at the heavy, bulky object she was struggling to hold in her hands. *Don't drop it,* she willed herself—this might be the kind of explosive that detonated on impact. *You can do this. You have to do this. You might not have gotten everyone into this mess, but it's up to you to get everyone out.*

She followed Lexi toward an emergency exit. In her jeans and sneakers—and not carrying a twenty-pound explosive device—Lexi was able to move a lot quicker. "How did you find me?" Brynn called out to her.

"I finally put all of this together, Brynn. I know what's going on."

So Lexi knew Jacob had made her build the bomb, then. Her hunch at the gym had been correct. Brynn was desperate to stop her friend and ask her how she'd confirmed that, but then her eyes fell to the timer. *Three forty-two. Three forty-one.*

"Lexi." She stopped. "There's no way we can get this out of here in time."

Lexi gestured to the stairs. "They've dug a foundation for a new building in the lot behind this one. We can throw it in there. It's not far."

Brynn groaned. "This thing might not look like much, but it's heavy. I doubt I can *throw* it."

Lexi stood on the landing. Her eyes darted back and forth. "What do you suggest we do instead?"

Brynn peered over the railing. Everyone drinking, eating, talking, smiling, laughing. A band had started to play, and the soldiers and their families were dancing. They had no idea what was going on up here. They were good people, honest people. They didn't deserve what was coming. She cursed herself for not calling the police earlier. All those fears about getting in trouble—what did it matter now if they were all going to die? She should have taken the fall. She should have seen the bigger picture.

Suddenly, she had an idea. It was the only idea, really. The only thing that would save them all. Hefting the bomb higher in her arms, she staggered to the landing and looked over.

"Hey!" she screamed. A few people looked up. Brynn held the bomb over her head. "Look!" she kept yelling. "Bomb! It's a bomb!"

"Are you *insane*?" Lexi screeched, trying to drag her back into the stairwell.

More people noticed. Jaws began to drop. Someone screamed. "She's got a *bomb*!" someone else bellowed.

"Hey!" Brynn kept calling. "Bomb!"

There was a mix of gasps, screams, and murmurs, and everyone started to run for the exit. The security guards aimed their guns at her, but Brynn just raised the bomb higher, and they backed off. She caught sight of her father's face—at first it was a mask of confusion, but then he looked desperate and terrified when he realized *she* was the one on the landing, making all this happen. "Brynn!" she heard him shout. He tried to push through the crowd to get to her.

"No!" Brynn screamed to him. "Get *out* of here! Now!"

And then she saw her mother, peering at her with such incomprehension she looked almost like a child. "Come on, come on!" someone said to Dr. Caldwell, shoving her toward an exit. Brynn's mother's eyes remained on her, though, even as she was pushed away.

A building alarm sounded, mixing with the mélange of screams. Red and blue flashing lights blinked from the ceiling and walls. From somewhere on the street, Brynn heard sirens. Footsteps thundered. The pandemonium was so great, everyone pushed to get out the atrium doors at once. Expensive handbags were left behind. Pretty high-heeled shoes. Half-eaten meals, half-drunk cocktails.

The bomb's timer continued to tick down.

Lexi was staring at her in horror. "Come on," Brynn said. She placed the bomb on the floor, square in the hall, then headed for the exit. "Everyone get out of here!" she called into the stairwell. "The bomb's going to blow in two minutes!" Security's footsteps stopped. Then they retreated.

Brynn's arms felt light without the device. Free. And they had two minutes to get safely away. One fifty-nine, one fifty-eight. She pushed through the metal emergency exit doors and hurried through a passageway to the back part of the BioXin campus. The building had cleared out. A door to a kitchen stood open, and pots bubbled on open flames, completely unattended. A water tap still ran. *One forty-seven, one forty-six ...*

An exit was ahead. Brynn pushed open the door and was relieved to see a dark mound of grass, dimly lit by a street-light. Brynn sprinted as hard as she could, only wanting to get as far from the bomb as possible. Lexi thundered behind her. They climbed the hill, passed a picnic table, and then almost tripped over a couple huddled in heavy jackets, out for a walk.

"Bomb!" Brynn screamed, gesturing for them to run in the opposite direction. The couple looked startled. The woman stared. *"Go!"* Brynn shouted, and they finally turned and hurried away.

Ninety seconds to go. *Eighty-nine. Eighty-eight.*

"We have to get as far away as we can," Brynn called to Lexi, remembering the physics report she'd done about outrunning an explosive. It felt so long ago now. Part of a simpler era. She thought about everyone else at the launch. Her mom. Her dad. Were they running, too? Would they survive this? Would they ever forgive her?

She heard shouts in the distance. Brynn glanced over her shoulder and saw a figure chasing her through the trees. "Stop!" a voice called. It had to be the police. Maybe they thought she still had the bomb. She kept running, figuring she'd talk to them after the explosion—if she lived. By her calculations, she had another thirty seconds to run. The figure continued to pursue, shrouded in darkness. *Twenty-one seconds. Twenty.*

"Brynn, I have to stop." Lexi's breathing was heavy. She collapsed on the grass. Brynn ran a few paces, then circled back. There was no way she could leave her friend.

"Okay," she said. "Get down."

They dropped to their stomachs, luckily shielded by the small hill. Brynn gazed at the BioXin building in the distance. The sun had set majestically behind it, bathing the structure in a pale orange glow.

All of a sudden, a fireball shot from the building's center. The sound was louder than anything Brynn had ever heard, and the force of it seemed to bubble up from the earth, lifting her from her spot on the grass and sending her airborne. Brynn was pretty sure she screamed, but the explosion was so deafening that all she could hear was an eerie ringing in her ears. She flew into the air and hit the ground again on her side, her teeth gnawing viciously into her cheek. She felt her head go limp on her neck and closed her eyes.

It was only a few moments before she opened them again. There was something sticky on her cheek, probably blood. Her leg felt mangled, but she was able to move her fingers and toes. Cautiously, she tried to sit. Lexi lay next to her on her back, her jeans covered in black streaks, her face covered in ash. Brynn crawled over to her friend and touched her arm. "Lexi. *Lexi!*"

Lexi's eyelids fluttered. The two girls stared at each other. Then Brynn turned. There was a cloud of black smoke where the BioXin building had stood. And beyond that, like a constant refrain, were wails and screams.

"Oh my God," Lexi whispered. Or at least it sounded like a whisper—Brynn was pretty sure her hearing had been affected by the blast. Lexi looked at something beyond Brynn, her eyes growing wide. Someone was standing over them.

It was a figure with cropped hair and narrowed eyes. He wore a green army jacket. Brynn didn't think he was a cop, but he was glaring at her with such disdain, such anger, that she felt her breath catch. As he stepped into the glow of the streetlight, which was somehow still functional, Brynn realized who it was. A small, sad part of her heart lifted when she saw him, but then she cowered back, horrified that he was real. *Here.*

"Oh, Brynn." He sounded perturbed. "Why did you have to be a do-gooder even to the end?"

Brynn swallowed. "I don't . . ."

"You weren't supposed to *warn* people," he said, his voice louder now, breaking through the cotton in Brynn's ears. "You did it all wrong."

"Wait a minute," Lexi rose to her knees. "Brynn saved *everyone.*"

He glanced at her with such an icy look that even Lexi shrank back a little. Brynn cleared her throat.

"Jacob," she said, her voice shaking, saying his name to him for the first time in ages, "g-get out of here. Don't come any closer."

Jacob blinked. A sickly, mirthless smile was spread across his lips. Only it was Lexi who spoke next. *"Jacob?"* She stared at Brynn as if Brynn had just caught on fire. "Brynn, that isn't Jacob."

Brynn let out a sad laugh. It seemed so late for introductions. "It is, Lexi. This is Jacob. My ex."

Lexi's eyes didn't leave Brynn's face. A muscle in her cheek twitched. "No, it *isn't.*" Her voice was haunted. Paralyzed. But also certain. "Brynn. That's *Dex.*"

TWENTY-EIGHT

Brynn felt weightless. Untethered to anything real. Lexi's mouth had moved, but she must have mistaken her friend's words. It was because of the bomb blast, the shock of the explosion. Her brain was scrambled, disintegrated, reduced to pulp.

But then Lexi said it again. "Brynn, that's Dex. Your *current* boyfriend. He goes to our *school*."

Brynn slowly turned back to the tall, leering figure standing among the rubble. Jacob's eyes blazed, but there was a smirk on his face, like he found all of this amusing. This was Jacob, through and through—the stiff way he held himself, how his gaze seemed to burn a hole in Brynn's confidence, even the way his hands were permanently curled into fists, as though he was always ready to throw a punch. Jacob still haunted her dreams. She'd be able to pick him out of a crowd of a million people. She'd be able to find him in the dark.

"You helped me build that bomb," she said to Jacob. "But *why?*"

"Because of his *brother*, Brynn!" Lexi cried desperately. "He's angry about his brother, Marc!"

Brynn blinked. "No. *Dex* has a brother named Marc. Not Jacob."

"They're the same *person*," Lexi urged.

Brynn stared at her. "Of course they're not."

"Okay, and what was Jacob's last name?" Lexi challenged.

Brynn frowned. Actually, she couldn't remember.

"It's Kinsley!" Lexi roared. "This is what Cortexia did to you! They injected you and then convinced you to *forget* Jacob! But he isn't *gone*. . . . He's still here. This is what I was trying to warn you about."

She whipped around and pointed an accusing finger at Jacob. "I figured it out. Figured *you* out. Some of my friends who got Cortexia injections in the clinical trials don't know reality from fantasy, either. And you knew about that, didn't you? Capitalized on it. Brynn mentioned to me that she was part of a plot she couldn't remember. She worried her old boyfriend was part of it. So I looked into this Jacob guy. Funny, Jacob's middle name is Dex. And both your last names are Kinsley."

Jacob rolled his eyes. "You have no idea what you're talking about."

"Lexi," Brynn said cautiously. Her voice sounded foreign and strained. "That's insane."

"Is it?" Lexi turned to Brynn. "He's a liar, Brynn. Just like he's always been. I should have told you the other day—*Dex* was the one who spoke badly of *you* at that restaurant. Said you were volatile. Angry. That I should stay away from you. I should have known something was wrong then. I should have told you."

Brynn's mouth fell open, but she didn't speak. The information rolled over her in waves, baffling but also sickeningly logical. Badmouthing her behind her back was something Jacob would do. And if Dex was Jacob . . .

She stared into Jacob's face. He *couldn't* be Dex. Dex was good. Kind.

But then Jacob dropped the sneer, and his expression turned neutral.

A horrifying jolt went through Brynn. It was Dex's face again. How could that *be*? She stared, sure it was a mirage, but no, there was Dex, looking at her blankly.

"Oh my God," she whispered.

Two different faces, two different beings inhabiting one body. It was completely disorienting. She touched her own cheeks, almost afraid they weren't still there, that the properties of the entire world had been turned on their head.

Lexi was pointing at Jacob again. "You banked on her

getting her memory wiped after the Cortexia injection and treatment. But then you reappeared in her life to make sure it all took."

"Shut *up*," Jacob hissed. He focused on Brynn. "It doesn't matter who I am. What matters is that it's over and done. The bomb went off. I wish you hadn't warned the whole world . . . but whatever."

Brynn blinked in horror. Dex's voice coming out of Jacob's mouth. She glanced at Lexi desperately. Her friend just raised her eyebrows as if to say, *See?*

"Oh my God." Brynn covered her mouth with her hands. She thought she might throw up. She fought hard to stay upright and on her feet. This was what had seemed off-kilter in her conversation with Lowell. *I know you've been together for a long time,* Lowell had said about Brynn and Dex. But she *hadn't* been with Dex for a long time, only a few months. But if Lowell knew Dex and Jacob as the same person . . .

"You," she whispered, pointing a shaky finger at him. *"You!"*

"You," Dex mocked, rolling his eyes. Brynn had never seen him roll his eyes at her before—that was something *Jacob* did. "You're so ridiculous, Brynn. I never thought you'd *tell* people about the bomb. You were just supposed to set it off and run. But you had to be the hero, didn't you? This brave new Brynn Caldwell, who thinks she can save the world."

A thin curl of smoke separated them, rising up from

some burnt and twisted piece of metal. It smelled noxious, but the strong sensation brought Brynn back to life. She gawked at him, mulling over his words.

"You wanted no one to know about the bomb? You wanted it to *kill* everyone?"

"Not everyone. The important people were already out of the building. I warned them about the bomb at the last minute, when I saw you go upstairs. I didn't think you'd remember what the activation meant. I just thought you'd panic and get the hell out of there—or even better, be so perplexed and flustered it would explode in your hands."

Brynn did a quick mental inventory. "But my mother was still in the atrium! I saw her after I activated it!"

"I was about to get to her," Dex said. "But I realized I needed to take care of you first."

His eyes were cold, unfeeling. Something he'd just said echoed in Brynn's mind. He wanted the bomb to explode in her hands. He wanted her *dead*.

"I don't understand," she said shakily. "I'm on your side, Dex."

Dex barked out a laugh. His smile was twisted, eerie. "Who says we're on the same side?"

Brynn blinked hard. "You're against Cortexia. Because of your brother. Because Cortexia *killed* him."

Dex looked at her pityingly. "Oh, Brynn. That's so sweet!"

Lexi shifted next to Brynn. In the sky, Brynn could

make out the *whap-whap-whap* of a helicopter's blades. And sirens, of course. So many sirens. There was something about Jacob's—Dex's—smile that was rehearsed, perfected, practically a clone of someone else's. Merriweather's smile, she realized with a start.

She was so shocked that she stumbled backwards. *Merriweather.* She'd wondered why his men had only half-heartedly chased Dex the day she'd found Lexi tied up. And it was why he'd insisted on taking the files Lowell had given Brynn, claiming he'd keep them safe. Dex had never intended to turn them in to a contact at the NSA. He'd probably shredded them by now.

"There is no ACL, is there?" she whispered. "You made it up. You pretended I'd joined. But it was just for you and me. It was so I'd follow you. Do whatever you wanted."

A final memory slotted into place: Brynn saw herself once again strapped to that chair, the Cortexia needle plunging into her arm. Just as she'd been given the injection, a door had burst open. Everyone turned as Jacob—for that was how she knew him, then—barreled into the room. *What are you doing with her?* Jacob screamed, pointing at Brynn in the chair.

Bruce Cress rounded on him. *Someone told her. We're not sure how. We heard her arguing with her mother. It's a train wreck.*

But I was using her! Jacob cried. I'm *the one who told her. I was trying to recruit her over to our side!*

Merriweather sniffed. *Well, you were careless. Because she talked.*

I told her not to, Jacob grumbled. He wiped his brow. *She would have been valuable. We could have used her as a bargaining tool, considering who her mother is.*

And then Merriweather stepped forward. *It's too late now.* He turned to Brynn. *See this guy? You don't remember him, and you don't want to. He was a jerk to you. He was manipulative and controlling and made you sad. So you don't even remember his full name, okay? Or his face.* The serum coursing through Brynn's bloodstream was so powerful and effective that all she could do was nod. *Yes. Yes. I will forget.*

A boom sounded, and Brynn tumbled back to reality. She gawked at Dex. Lexi had told her about friends who'd killed themselves because of Cortexia, but Jacob's story had driven the point home. He'd described his brother's death and suicide. He'd explained how the results had been buried. He'd pleaded with Brynn to help him with his cause. Of course she'd jumped at the chance—she did anything for Jacob. So then she must have gone to her mother . . . and Lowell . . . and her mother called that meeting with the board of directors. That's when Brynn was given Cortexia. Dr. Caldwell, too.

Jacob, meanwhile, disappeared . . . and reemerged as Dex, the sweet boy who sat next to her in physics. The shoulder she cried on. The boy who changed her life. This time, he made it out like Marc's death had been an accident.

He kept their secret plot under wraps. He slowly fed it to Brynn through those texts, selectively hinting at pieces of her memory until they returned. The most important thing hadn't returned: that *he* had been in on it. That he'd been Jacob. That he was *still* manipulating her.

But that wasn't the most shocking part. What was most shocking was how familiarly Dex spoke to those men in that room. Cress, Merriweather—they were part of this plan, too. All of a sudden, it made sense. "You're on the same team as Merriweather," she whispered to him. "You don't want Cortexia gone. You want it to flourish. You and Merriweather want to *brainwash* everyone."

"I admire what Merriweather is trying to do." Dex puffed out his chest. "I want to brainwash the terrorists. It's because of them that my brother went to that godforsaken place, and it's because of them that he came back a ghost." He spit out the words. "If there's a way I can get rid of their way of thinking for good, then of course I'm going to support that."

"But, Dex!" Brynn cried. "What if it doesn't stop at terrorists? What if it goes much further? You and I *talked* about this. It's the ultimate weapon!"

Dex shrugged. "All the more reason it should be in the hands of a real American like Merriweather—someone who's not afraid to use it."

"Did Merriweather tell you to build that bomb?" Lexi cried.

"Not exactly." Dex turned to her. "But I knew he wanted me to do it. It's the only way we could show the world how exposed all of us are to terrorism, and to put Cortexia at the center of that. The bomb goes off at the launch, people are killed, your mother has no choice but to turn over the patent to allow our government to use it—and whatever force necessary—to keep terrorists at bay." He looked at Brynn. "That's how it was *supposed* to go. But now the death toll is much lower. Still a success, though."

Brynn's mind was reeling. "B-But when we found the bomb, you told me to turn myself in! And then you said *you'd* turn me in if I didn't!"

His grin was sinister. "It was all about testing you—and scaring you. You were so afraid of being busted that I knew you wouldn't go to the authorities about any of it. I knew you'd do exactly what I wanted."

Brynn stared into his eyes. His pupils were small. His irises were opaque, bottomless. There was no love there. He'd never cared for her. At the same time, there was a wobble in his mouth she remembered, the same twitch he always got when talking about Marc. She had to believe his depth of feeling for his brother was real, but how had he become so misguided? Then again, he was Jacob, not Dex—and Jacob *was* misguided. Manipulative. Diabolical. It felt like her heart was breaking into pieces, but she had to ignore that for now. She had to focus on her hate for this person. Her mistrust. Her anger at what he'd done.

She turned away from him, wiping smoke out of her eyes. "I'm not doing what you want anymore," she said, fully aware of the power she still had. "My mother will never give up her patent. And pretty soon, everyone's going to know the truth."

Dex snorted. "Doubtful."

Brynn reached into her pocket for her phone. Thankfully, it was still intact, the screen only mildly cracked from her fall. She pulled up a PDF file she'd stored in a folder and swiftly attached it to a list of email recipients she'd put together before heading off to the launch. There were names from the *New York Times*. The *Washington Post*. Papers in Los Angeles, Chicago. Major news networks as well as affiliates overseas. Rainer Wilson from *Newsnight*. It wasn't like Brynn knew any of them personally, but someone in their camp would read the email and realize its importance.

"I scanned those files before giving them to you," she said.

The blood drained from Dex's face. *"What?"*

"Yep. All of them. Every last one. At the time, I didn't know why ... but I guess I have my answer. Something in the back of my brain told me not to trust you." She smiled. "I guess they were right when they said Cortexia acts differently on teenage minds, huh?"

Dex's nostrils flared. "You *bitch.*"

He lunged at her. Brynn ducked away, her finger hovering over Send. As she pressed it, she felt a force at her back. Something whipped her to the right, and suddenly she was on the ground, her hands pinned behind her. Her cell phone skittered into a pile of loose bricks. Brynn could see it vaguely glowing through the cracks.

"It was her, officer!" Dex shouted, eagerly pressing all of his weight onto her spine. "I've got her! She's the one who built the bomb!"

Brynn heard footsteps. Several cops surrounded her now, their guns drawn. "I was trying to *save* everyone!" she called weakly. "I swear!"

"She's right!" Lexi shouted. "He's the person you should worry about!" She jabbed a finger at Dex, but suddenly Brynn saw her head snap back and her legs buckle. Lexi crumpled to the ground without another word.

"Lexi!" Brynn screeched. She struggled to see who'd just knocked Lexi over. "What did you *do*?"

"Quiet," the cop holding Brynn growled. Brynn stared at his profile. The sunset made a golden glow around his head. The wispy clouds and pinkish-orange light looked beautiful, and Brynn could almost imagine that she wasn't lying in a pile of ruins behind a bombed-out building. The man handcuffing her might have been wearing a security uniform, but it bore a BioXin logo on the breast pocket. She thought of Lowell's words. *They're among us, Brynn.*

Watching. Slowly, he reached for something in his pocket. It was an oblong pouch. The Velcro made a sticky sound as he undid it and pulled out a syringe.

Brynn's stomach flipped over.

"No," she whispered, shrinking back. The syringe shone in the dying sunlight. There was a delighted grin on his face as he flicked the tip and the tiniest drop of Cortexia dripped out.

"No!" Brynn cried, tears filling her eyes. This couldn't happen again. She couldn't forget this. She needed to *remember.*

She thrashed against the man, but he easily pinned her down and rolled up her sleeve. In the moment before he plunged the needle into her arm, Dex swam into view beyond him. Their eyes met briefly, but Dex no longer looked angry. His Adam's apple rose as he swallowed. "I'm sorry, Brynn," he said steadily. "I hope that, after all this is over, we can still be friends."

Brynn stared at him emptily. Moments ago, she would have felt touched. Moments ago, she would have reached out for him, wanting Dex and only Dex to shepherd her through this horrible trial. But it was freeing, in a way, to know the truth. It would be the only bright spot in receiving Cortexia again, she realized. She wouldn't have to remember him. She wouldn't have to remember this pain. Not at all.

But everyone else would. Because those files were out

there. And they would lead back to the people who deserved to go down. Justice would be done, and that was all that really mattered.

"You're dead to me," she growled at Dex, turning her head away. She braced herself for the needle's sting, but in the end, she didn't even feel it. She was already gone.